CW00829604

WORLD WAR III

America's Last Stand

James Silvia

INFINITY
PUBLISHING

All rights reserved. No part of this book shall be reproduced or transmitted in any form or by any means, electronic, mechanical, magnetic, photographic including photocopying, recording or by any information storage and retrieval system, without prior written permission of the publisher. No patent liability is assumed with respect to the use of the information contained herein. Although every precaution has been taken in the preparation of this book, the publisher and author assume no responsibility for errors or omissions. Neither is any liability assumed for damages resulting from the use of the information contained herein.

Copyright © 2014 by James Silvia

ISBN 978-0-7414-7346-2
ISBN 978-0-7414-7347-9 eBook

Printed in the United States of America

Published November 2014

INFINITY PUBLISHING
1094 New DeHaven Street, Suite 100
West Conshohocken, PA 19428-2713
Toll-free (877) BUY BOOK
Local Phone (610) 941-9999
Fax (610) 941-9959
Info@buybooksontheweb.com
www.buybooksontheweb.com

For Melissa

Developing a strong will to learn and common sense to apply overtime creates a lifelong work well remembered.

INTRODUCTION

Within these pages is the result of soul searching and biblical research. It has been a lifelong passion of mine to learn the end time prophecies. To plainly understand which methods God will use to usher in the eagerly anticipated last days. The challenge was how to obtain a clear perception. As the years passed, many disappointments mounted. The quest for knowledge grew into a strengthening personal desire to learn the truth. After years of frustration in the perplexity of solitary research my spirit was awakened to seek the Lord. And what was learned is quite a tale to be told.

Gazing with spiritually sound discernment, the veil concealing the mysterious Babylon's true identity has been lifted. Astounded over many eye opening revelations and countless modern day earth changing and historical events that appear to revolve around her, in fact developed and shaped daily life sits the modern Babylon at the top center stage of the world. The truth of mankind's prophetic future I have come to realize is gripping and compelling in its fearsome scope and detail fulfilling numerous prophecies with more to come.

There is insight into chosen books of the Holy Bible (both the King James Version and the Modern Translation) including the Antichrist and the Mark of the Beast. Quatrains of Nostradamus have also been carefully selected painting a prophetic picture of the near future that few understand. Materializing world events to the careful observer appear as intensifying

signs flashing out their warnings of terrible tribulations and disasters soon to come. What I see today are many dark storm clouds gathering on the horizon. And in the post 9-11 era which we now live, I felt compelled to rewrite a portion of my memoirs concerning the coming Great Tribulation (or "The Great Purification" known to many Native Indian Tribes) due to the heighten sense of urgency. The world as we know it is running out of precious time.

SIGNS OF THE LAST DAYS

2 Timothy 3:1-5 (New International Version) - "There will be terrible times in the last days. People will be lovers of themselves, lovers of money, boastful, proud, abusive, disobedient to their parents, ungrateful, unholy, without love, unforgiving, slanderous, without self-control, brutal, not lovers of the good, treacherous, rash, conceited, lovers of pleasure rather than lovers of God – having a form of godliness but denying its power. Have nothing to do with such people."

Luke 17:26-27 (Modern Translation) - "When I return the world will be as indifferent to the things of God as the people were in Noah's day. The ate and drank and married-everything just as usual right up to the day when Noah went into the ark and the flood came and destroyed them all."

Luke 17:28-30 (Modern Translation) - "And the world will be as it was in the days of Lot: people went about their daily business-eating and drinking, buying and selling, farming and building until the morning Lot left Sodom. Then fire and brimstone rained down from

heaven and destroyed them all. Yes, it will be 'business as usual' right up to the hour of my return."

Matthew 24:4-8 (King James Version) - "And Jesus answered and said unto them, Take heed that no man deceive you. For many shall come in my name, saying I am Christ; and shall deceive many. And ye shall hear of wars and rumors of wars; see that ye be not troubled; for all these things must come to pass, but the end is not yet. For nation shall rise against nation, and kingdom against kingdom; and there shall be famines, and pestilences, and earthquakes, in divers places. All these are the beginning of sorrows."

Matthew 24:9-13 (Modern Translation) - "Then you will be tortured and killed and hated all over the world because you are mine, and many of you shall fall back into sin and betray and hate each other. And many false prophets will appear and lead many astray. Sin will be rampant everywhere and will cool the love of many. But those enduring to the end shall be saved."

2 Thessalonians 2:3 (Modern Translation) - "Don't be carried away and deceived regardless of what they say. For that day will not come until two things happen: first, there will be a time of great rebellion against God, and then the "man" of rebellion will come-the son of hell."

I Thessalonians 5:3 (Modern Translation) – "When people are saying, "All is well, everything is quiet and peaceful" – then, all of a sudden, disaster will fall upon them as suddenly as a woman's birth pains begin when her child is born. And these people will not be able to get away anywhere – there will be no place to hide."

CONTENTS

THE LORD GRANTS WISDOM

Isaiah 8:19 (Modern Translation) - "So why are you trying to find out the future by consulting witches and mediums? Don't listen to their whisperings and mutterings. Can the living find out the future from the dead? Why not ask your God?"

Nostradamus (written in a letter to his eldest son, Cesar): "I do not say, my son...that future, very distant things cannot be known by any reasonable creature: on the contrary, the intellectually minded person is well able to perceive things both present and far-off provided that these are not too utterly occult or obscure. But the perfect appreciation of things cannot be acquired without that divine inspiration, given that all prophetic inspiration takes its prime moving principle first from God the creator, then from fortune and instinct."

Edgar Casey (The sleeping prophet): "I do not believe there is a single individual that does not possess this same ability I have, if they would be willing to pay the price of detachment of self- interest that it takes to develop those abilities."

Throughout history man in his search to gain knowledge of the future, corrupted himself to create and practice numerous rituals. In these endless attempts few have prayed in the name of the Lord for understanding. Matthew 21:22 (Modern Translation) -

"You can get anything-anything you ask for in prayer-if you believe." Even the prophet Daniel fasted and prayed for understanding.

It has been my own experience we forge our own chains of sin one link at a time. The reason a scarce number achieved the miracle in understanding the biblical scriptures is the very same reason multitudes have perished. Few possess knowledge of God. Satan (the father of all lies) has skillfully created endless diversions and vanity. Suffering from their own ignorance many insist on living in the foolish consistency of denial which eventually leads to a prison of their own making. Captivating and afflicting a vast majority of the population sin forces its conquered slaves to wander aimlessly in dismay. People in such a mental state generally tend to make unwise and or hasty decisions. Aggravating and deepening their sorrows. Leading too many stress related illnesses causing the misery and death of untold numbers. The age old strategy of evil is to divide and conquer. Too destroy from within. However, through our Lord Jesus Christ God breaks the chains of bondage to set us free. And for all of you who can hear do not squander anymore precious time by allowing yourself to become a victim of your own carelessness.

A word to the wise: Ralph Waldo Emerson wrote: "Do not follow where the path may lead. Go, instead where there is no path and leave a trail." The experience (which in itself brings for knowledge) of praying for understanding combined with profound continual study and research of the holy scriptures for clear insight opens up a whole new world of knowledge and wisdom. What people throughout history have failed to understand is that the Holy Bible was written to serve mankind. At an early age Michel de Nostradamus

(Latin translation from Nostradame December 21, 1503 – July 2, 1566) and Edgar Casey (March 18, 1877 – January 3, 1945) began to discover studying the Old and New Testament, pure genuine power dwells from within. To meditate, practice and maintain each day so you may spiritually mature inside heaven's set boundary suitable to sustain a growing personal relation with God. In time one may begin to understand and to appreciate the treasure trove of inherited riches buried deep within. Life has taught preparation takes self-sacrifice and steadfast determination. So be on the lookout of the things that can destroy all the good you start. Remain strong and of good faith, you never know who you are inspiring. The truth my friends holds a healing power all of its own.

The Solitary Path Leads To Great Discovery

Proverbs 2:1-6 (Modern Translation) - "Every young man who listen to me and obeys my instructions will be given wisdom and good sense. Yes, if you want better insight and discernment and are searching for them as you would for lost money or hidden treasure, then wisdom will be given you and knowledge of God himself; you will soon learn the importance of reverence for the Lord and of trusting him. For The Lord Grants Wisdom."

Acts 2:38 (Modern Translation) - "And Peter replied, each one of you must turn from sin, return to God and be baptized in the name of Jesus Christ for the forgiveness of your sins; then you also shall receive this gift the Holy Spirit."

Galatians 5:22-23 (Modern Translation) - "But when the Holy Spirit controls our lives he will produce this kind of fruit in us: love, joy, peace, patience, kindness, goodness, faithfulness, gentleness, and self-control; and here there is no conflict with Jewish laws."

1 Corinthians 14:1 (Modern Translation) - "Let love be your greatest aim; nevertheless, ask also for the special abilities the Holy Spirit gives, especially the ability to prophecy."

Matthew 12:31 (Modern Translation) - "Even blasphemy against me or any other sin can be forgiven- all except one: speaking against the Holy Spirit shall never be forgiven, either in this world or in the world to come."

James 1:5-8 (Modern Translation) - "If you want to know what God wants you to do, ask him, and he will gladly tell you, for he is always ready to give a bountiful supply of wisdom to all who ask him; he will not resent it. But when you ask him, be sure that you really expect him to tell you, for a doubtful mind will be as unsettled as a wave of the sea that is driven and tossed by the wind; and every decision you then make will be uncertain, as you turn first this way, and then that. If you don't ask with faith, don't expect the Lord to give you any solid answer."

Matthew 7:7-8 (Modern Translation) - "Ask, and you will be given what you ask for. Seek, and you will find. Knock, and the door will be opened. For everyone who asks, receives. Anyone who seeks finds. If only you will knock, the door will open.

Babylon's Identity

The identity of the mysterious Babylon is the most valuable prophetic discovery in modern times since the Jews return to the holy land. The Lord not only revealed an ancient prophecy. He reaffirmed my faith. Within Revelation chapters seventeen and eighteen, Jeremiah chapters fifty and fifty one, Isaiah chapter forty seven describes the Mighty and Mysterious Babylon. These five chapters were used as a hammer of understanding to break down the ancient wall of obscurity.

Empires throughout history have made lasting impressions upon the world. Specifically two empires as Rome and Egypt were once magnificent wonders. Nevertheless their time has passed. In the 21st century, the past is made present. The future Babylon the Great, the modern Roman Empire, and colorful commercialized Sodom and Gomorrah spiritually resembles a candid and vivid reflection to the superpower United States of America.

The definition of apostate: *one who renounces his religion or his party; false; traitorous.* History proves early warning signs of a people falling prey to the blinding spell of apostate is a spiritual and moral decline. The cause of such degenerate behavior originates when a people choose to place their own personal gain ahead of guiding principles.

THE GREAT NEW CITY

There is controversy surrounding the identity of this mysterious Babylon. Many are misguided or argue the literal point that America is a nation and not a city. The modern Babylon is in fact "The Great New City." The definition of great: *of vast power and excellence; eminent; majestic.* The definition of new: *recent in origin; not before known; different; unaccustomed; fresh after any event.* The definition of city: *a large town; a borough or town corporate.* The definition of borough: *a town with municipal government.* The definition of municipal: *belonging to a corporation or city.* The definition of corporate: *formed into a legal body; and empowered to act in legal processes as an individual.* Within the times of ancient Greece their existed what was termed "city states." The isolated valleys and rough mountain terrain including the small islands scattered in the Mediterranean ocean inspired the creation of the city states with each one made up of an independent city self-governing, and self-sustaining. Two such city states were Athens known for their higher education in literature and science then Sparta for their military strength. With these age old ideals the American Empire clearly mimics the political landscape of ancient Greece. For example: The Great State of New York. Within the state boundaries are many towns and cities with one major metropolitan area known as "The Greater New York," which consists of five major towns, Manhattan, The Bronx, Brooklyn, Queens and Staten Island have through time and progress merged together to create and maintain their own municipal government. And each independent American State by political definition allowed according to the U.S.

Constitution to retain its sovereignty with its own State Government.

A union of City States with the ever-increasing educated population explosion and a global economy designed to grow and expand, the routine of steady management personal and business wealth building to include the investments of time and money into the enormous complexity of advanced technological research and development, has been laying the foundation of boundless growth and urban development. Creating and evolving into "the Great New City." Without hesitation there is no city, kingdom or nation in relation to the five biblical chapters listed above with striking detail other than America.

Jeremiah 50:32 (Modern Translation) - "Land of pride, you will stumble and fall and no one will raise you up, for the Lord will light a fire in the cities of Babylon that will burn everything around them." The scripture describes Babylon's "cities" will be destroyed by fire. A collection of cities created and united together under one system of governmental law creates a nation. Babylon, The Great New City is the United States - the land of pride. Clearly it was not the biblical descriptions alone and or the process of eliminating the possibilities among the nations to see which would be fit to wear the crown. It was by the wisdom of the Holy Spirit that brought sound judgment to my mind.

Throughout history walls were put in place to protect and fortify a city from invasion by foreign powers. Today, in a world wide scale, the United States has through a gradual nevertheless painstaking process created a similar fortification. Identical to the Roman Empire, America extends beyond her borders

by way of political and military expansion to protect the homeland. America has authority buildings and military bases the world over to safeguard vital U.S. interests.

It was the suggestion of President Herbert Clark Hoover (August 10, 1874 - October 20, 1964) to establish a plan titled "Fortress America" a shield of sea and air power in both oceans. In the post-world war II era, it was a strategic plan envisioned by General Douglas MacArthur (January 26, 1880 – April 5, 1964) to strengthen the defenses of the "Pax Americana." The upgraded plan would envision a shield of sea and air power to defend against the rising threats not just to North America, the entire Western Hemisphere. This shield blends in with the defense lines or walls. These walls are outposts where American and allied forces are housed. The strategic plans intertwined together have not only become reality, the endless preparations in all fields over time has grown and evolved more complex.

Nostradamus also described a "Great New City" destroyed by fire. Scholars of the quatrains agree when Nostradamus wrote of "New City" he was referring to the cities in the new world of America.

Century X, Quatrain 49:
Garden of the World <u>near</u> the New City,
in the <u>way</u> of the man-made mountains,
shall be <u>seized</u> on and <u>plunged</u> into a ferment,
being forced to drink sulphurous poisoned waters.

Century VI, Quatrain 97:
The heaven <u>shall</u> burn at five and forty degrees,
the fire <u>shall</u> come <u>near</u> the Great New City,
in an instant a great flame dispersed <u>shall</u> burst out,
<u>when</u> they <u>shall</u> make a <u>trial</u> of the Normans.

The definition of near: *not in a distant place, time or degree; close to; intimate.* The Great New City dwells in a paradise named: North America - the Garden of the World. The two are intimate and have become one power. Abraham Lincoln (February 12, 1809 – April 15, 1865) in his speech at the young men's Lyceum of Springfield Illinois on January 27, 1838 once said: "We find ourselves in the peaceful possession of the fairest portion of the earth as regards of extent of territory, fertility of soil and salutary of climate." The definition of way: *A track, path or road of any kind; progress; direction; course; method; line of business.* The man-made mountains (hollow mountains described by scholars) or modern skyscrapers and other high rise buildings of all shapes and sizes track the identical direction and course of progress or line of business within North America with perfect intimacy. And according to all known prophecy will be seized on and plunged into a terrible ferment. The definition of seize: *to lay hold of suddenly; to take by force; to attack.* The definition of plunge: *to thrust or push; to immerse.* The definition of thrust: *to push or drive with force; to shove.* The United States political, economic and strategic military methods and practices over the years have caused endless worldwide controversy inevitably adding up to one course of action. For America's enemies to seize or suddenly attack with a nuclear ferment and take by force the Great New City in all-out war. With the survivors forced to drink poisoned contaminated waters.

The definition of shall: *future tense.* The heavens or skies shall burn due to the tremendous rising heat filled with burning ambers for the nations to witness. Nostradamus gave details as to where the burning skies would be located. Scholars of the quatrains

have believed the five and forty degrees refer to forty five degrees in latitude. Scholars also agree when Nostradamus wrote the particular quatrain it reveals the "Great New City" as New York City. Nevertheless I believe the scholars to be partially correct. Observing more closely the forty five degree latitude directly extends not only through northern New York State. It extends parallel the entire length of the American and Canadian border. The Great New City located near forty five degrees in latitude shall become devoured by a great flame dispersed and burst out. The definition of disperse: *to scatter; to dispel.* The definition of dispel: *to fly in different ways.*

The definition of when: *At what or which or while; whereas; used substantively with since.* The definition of while: *A time; short space of time; during the time.* The definition of trial: *examination by test; judicial examination.* During the creation of an anticipated trial the Scarlet Animal and his ten horns proclaim themselves judge, jury and executioner while isolating and destroying the Normans or Western allies.

"The Normans were Viking raiders from Northern Europe in the ninth century known as Norsemen or North-men. The North-men loved the sea, and were involved in many raids and trades along the French (Frankish Kingdom) coast. Leading to commercial prosperity the Norsemen grew to considerable wealth and power. In an effort to stop the plundering, Frankish King Charles offered a large piece of land in northern France to the North-men in return for their obedience to the Frankish crown. The land was settled and named Normandy. Gradually over the course of time the name North-men/Norsemen changed to the Normans."

"The Normans conquered the lands of England, Sicily and Italy. And were the force behind the

Crusades. The city of Normandy was eventually conquered by the French King Phillip II. Many of the surviving Norman people who lived in the conquered lands blended in with the native peoples adapting the language and culture through marriage. Inevitably the future children of those bloodlines sailed to the new world."

Beauty and the Beast

Beauty

Revelation 17:9 (King James Version) - "And here is the mind which hath wisdom. The seven heads are seven mountians, on which the woman sitteth."

Revelation 17:15 (Modern Translation) - "The oceans, lakes and rivers that the woman is sitting on represent masses of people of every race and nation."

Revelation 17:3-4 (Modern Translation) - "So the angel took me in spirit into the wilderness. There I saw a woman sitting on a scarlet animal that had seven heads and ten horns, written all over with blasphemies against God. The woman wore purple and scarlet clothing and beautiful jewelry made of gold and precious gems and pearls, and held in her hand a golden goblet full of obscenities."

"Amerigo Vespucci was an Italian explorer and cartographer (March 9, 1451 - February 22, 1512) of the new South American continent. However, it was accepted the two new continents named

after the explorer. German cartographers Martin Waldseemuller and Matthias Ringmann drawing up a world map decided on the latinized version: Amerious Vespucius. The feminine name derived from the latinized version which is "America."

Three separate scriptures in which the modern woman America is sitting upon her throne with each scripture proceeding into further detail than the last. The first: the modern woman sitting upon the seven mountains or seven continents of the world. The second: the woman sits upon all bodies of water of every size waters or multitudes of people from every race and nation. The third: reveals the modern woman America sitting upon the Scarlet Animal with seven heads and ten horns. The Scarlet Animal is the Antichrist and his ten horn or ten king alliance. The seven heads represent seven kings of the past. Antichrist is one of those seven kings. The golden goblet in her hand is the symbolic meaning of great wealth. This may also be said by her beautiful jewelry and clothing. The appearance of tremendous wealth also describes her as a seductress.

The luring array of bright beautiful colors with her precious jewelry and the golden cup reveals the harlot's attractive lifestyle in view of the whole earth. Her refreshing presence renewing the ages of endless possibilities is a magnificent feast for the blind sore eyes. With lavish seductions of great wealth lure many away from God. With numbers having died pursuing their full share of obtainable material riches. There is however another hidden mystery to the brilliant colors of purple and scarlet clothing (having a close relation with the golden cup and precious jewelry) I have uncovered. The definition of scarlet: *a bright-red color; of a bright red color; offensive*. The definition of Of: *denoting source; cause; motive; possession; quality;*

condition; material; concerning; relating to; about. The definition of offensive: *highly irritating; angering; annoying.* The definition of irritate: *annoying or provoking.* The scarlet red clothing the modern woman possesses relates and reveals her sinful and immoral works highly offensive and provoking. Angering and irritating many with her annoying comfortable controlling and hypocritical presence. The definition of purple: *a color produced by mixing red and blue; regal power; a color made of red and blue; dyed with blood.* The definition of dye: *to stain; to give a new and permanent color to; tinge.* The definition of regal: *to refresh sumptuously; to feast; a splendid feast; a treat.* The definition of refresh: *to revive; to reanimate; to freshen.* The definition of sumptuous: *very expensive or costly; splendid; magnificent.* Deep purple as it is known today imperial purple. The definition of imperial: *pertaining to an empire or emperor; supreme; suitable for an emperor of superior excellence.* Roman Emperors and other forms of royalty have indeed worn these very colors in their costly, splendid and magnificent rise to power. Colors of blue and red mixed together create the color purple. The purple linen is stained with hidden scarlet or blood red, the many sins of murder and other fowl crimes written all over her against God. The harlot's clothing reveals and conceals her sins.

The myth of gems it may influence the spirit of the wearer. The definition of influence: *agency or power serving to affect; modify; sway; effect; acknowledged; bias; ascendency with people in power.* "The magic and beauty gems have a vast heritage of healing power. Known to cure, heal and protect." Nevertheless gems also have an influential way all their own to sway and modify the mind and spirit into the controlling grip of wealth, power and idol worship. The ancient Greeks

and Romans had "a close connected view of pearls and marriage." The mixture of gold fever, gems and pearls cut and created her to a high rare quality of remarkable perfection and precious radiant beauty. Well known worldwide for her pearls of wisdom and knowledge of human reasoning. Including the gems her vast fortunes and healing powers. She has glorified herself in the acceptance of steadfast marriage, security health and wealth to all nations who receive her. The ornaments of precious jewelry, gold and fine clothing reveals not only who she is and what she has become. It reveals these assorted luxuries obviously are her.

Jeremiah 51:6-7 (Modern Translation) - "Babylon has been as a gold cup in the Lord's hands, a cup from which he made the whole earth drink and go mad." Revelation 17:2 (Modern Translation) - "The kings of the world have had immoral relations with her, and the people of the earth have been made drunk by the wine of her immorality." Revelation 17:6 (Modern Translation) - "I could see that she was drunk-drunk with the blood of the martyrs of Jesus she had killed. I stared at her in horror." Blood drunk from the endless sacrifices which paved the wide open road for her continual overflowing abundance of great wealth, power and promise of intoxicating success, a desired whore of leisure with endless legal and illegal business and or trade agreements in existence with the peoples of the earth and their leaders who have become obsessed to the point that cannot be reasonably described with material riches. Turning from the truth many have fallen prey to the idol power of their earthly wealth causing them to spiritually fall into a deeper more drunken slumber of denial.

The modern woman America is also known as the Queen Kingdom of the world (Isaiah 47:7). The President of the United States or King of the South (Daniel 11:40) is also known as the King of Babylon (Jeremiah 50:43). In accordance with tradition each President or King is in temporary marriage to the the modern woman or Queen Kingdom. And they both sit upon the highest and most powerful throne within all the earth.

THE BEAST

Revelation 17:3-4 (Modern Translation) - "So the angel took me in spirit into the wilderness. There I saw a woman sitting on a scarlet animal that had seven heads and ten horns, written all over with blasphemies against God. The woman wore purple and scarlet clothing and beautiful jewelry made of gold and precious gems and pearls, and held in her hand a golden goblet full of obscenities."

Revelation 17:10-11 (Modern Translation) - "They also represent seven kings. Five have fallen, the sixth now reigns and the seventh is yet to come, but his reign will be brief. The Scarlet Animal that died is the eighth king, having reigned before as one of the seven; after his second reign, he too will go to his doom."

Two scriptures reveal a scarlet animal. The reason for the scarlet or bright red color his soul is deeply stained with sin. The scarlet animal is without a doubt the Antichrist, the man of power, the god of technology. A mysterious man who once lived as one of the seven kings of history, will rise from the pits of hell and live

again as the eighth king or Scarlet Animal. And reign as the chosen son of Satan. After his second reign the Scarlet Beast will go to his eternal doom. The ten horns are ten modern day kings or leaders who will agree to an alliance with the Antichrist. The evil obscene blasphemies written all over insulting to God reveal centuries of hard brutal work and endless sacrifices went into the creation of today's vast turbulent technologically advanced civilization which in fact is a worldwide empire of idol worship created from evil's deceitful influence all in the name of progress to devour the entire earth.

Revelation 13:1-2 (Modern Translation) - "And now, in my vision, I saw a Strange Creature rising up out of the sea. It had seven heads and ten horns and ten crowns upon its horns. And written on each head were blasphemous names, each one defying and insulting God. This Creature looked like a leopard but had bear's feet and a lion's mouth! And the Dragon gave him his own power and throne and great authority." The scripture is revealing more detail. In this vision the Strange Creature is rising up out of the sea of nations, the very same waters the modern woman America is sitting upon. Why is the Strange Creature rising up out of the sea? The moment Antichrist creates the alliance with these ten selected kings or heads of state. The Scarlet Animal and his Strange Ten Horn Wild Beast will have been given birth catapulting the Antichrist to power of unimaginable heights. Providing the prophetical finishing touches upon the Strange Creature of Revelation 13:1-2 the insurrection above all the seas of nations but one the United States. She is sitting upon all-the world, and this includes the Strange Creature. The crown upon each of the ten

horns is evident they are kings or heads of state. The ten horns briefly, the Antichrist's prepared and highly motivated weapons of attack. The Dragon (Satan) has given his son Antichrist his own power, throne and great authority. Satan's spirit of influence works from within the Antichrist. Antichrist's power is satanic and not his own (Daniel 8:24). Driven by Satan's powerful influence to deceive and imprison the entire globe.

In these last days which we live all mankind's sins of the past appears to be resurfacing in a devilishly inspired and cleverly orchestrated haunting repeat of history. And all the modern worldwide illuminating sense of false security from the influential satanic deceit has basically given birth to this ultimate evil inspired and man-made creation. Over its short life span as the power and influence of the Strange Wild Creature increases, its works dangerously insulting toward God will become more dramatic and defiled. And will intensify the Lord's anger greatly. It is nothing more than a vicious cycle that is escalating its way toward worldwide spiritual disaster and all-out war.

Daniel's Six Beasts

The First Beast

Daniel 7:4 (King James Version) - "The first was like a lion, and had eagle's wings: I beheld till the wings thereof were plucked, and it was lifted up from the earth, and made stand upon the feet as a man, and a man's heart was given to it."

Daniel 7:4 (Modern Translation) - "The first was like a lion, but it had eagle's wings! And as I watched, its wings were pulled off so that it could no longer fly, and it was left standing on the ground, on two feet, like a man; and a man's mind was given to it."

Daniel 7:4 (New International Version) - "The first was like a lion, and it had the wings of an eagle. I watched until its wings were torn off and it was lifted from the ground so that it stood on two feet like a human being, and the mind of a human was given to it."

In his dream Daniel witnessed a fierce storm over a turbulent ocean as one by one, four mighty beasts began rising up. The raging waters represent the troubled and restless modern sea of nations. The first beast represents the western alliance. The beast is a lion, and not a woman. Why? England's symbol of the lion represents majestic strength and power. Ezekiel 38:13 (King James Version) - "Tarshish, with all the young lions, seek to plunder." In ancient times one way

to trade goods was through ships. Many merchants got their tin from Tarshish. There is an old saying: "Britannia rules the waves, England the mistress of the seas." Britannia (Britain) means the land of tin. England is symbolized by the mother lion. And yet Ezekiel said: "Tarshish with all the young lions." The young lions are the English speaking nations of the earth, including the United States and Canada.

The three scriptures of the eagle's wings plucked, pulled or torn off and then a man's heart and or mind given walk hand in hand. Isaiah 47:10 (Modern Translation) - "You felt secure in all your wickedness. No one sees me, you said. Your "wisdom" and "knowledge" have caused you to turn away from me and claim that you yourself are Jehovah." Within her own ambitious house of secrecy in pursuit of more knowledge America bears many burdens of responsibility against God's divine laws which the Lord is holding her accountable.

In the above scripture is the modern translation of Daniel 7:4. In it, the eagle's wings were "pulled" off. The definition of pull: *to draw towards one; to tug; to rend.* The definition of rend: *to tear away; to force asunder.* The definition of asunder: *apart; in a divided state.* In the King James Version of the same scripture the word "pluck" is used. The definition of pluck: *to pick; to pull sharply; to reject as failing in a examination.* The definition of reject: *to cast off; to discard; to repel; to forsake; to decline.* Piecing it all together makes it abundantly clear. In this modern highly evolved civilization the entire western kingdoms are falling prey to the one condemning fate that has claimed so many other kingdoms and empires of the past a divided and declining state while their enemies continue to strengthen in numbers, talents and

capabilities. Matthew 12:25 (Modern Translation) - "Jesus knew their thoughts and replied, "A divided kingdom ends in ruin. A city or home divided against it-self cannot stand."

In the Modern Translation of Daniel 7:4, a man's mind was given. The definition of mind: ***intellectual power in a man; understanding, inclination*****. The definition of inclination:** ***deviation from a normal direction; a leaning of the mind or will; tendency; bent; bias*****. The definition of deviation:** ***a turning aside from the right away, course or line*****. America in her actions is silently proclaiming she is a self-made god while deviate leaning her mind and will toward the corruptible and blinding power of knowledge and wisdom, instead of the knowledge and wise path of God. America from her beginning has had that lone ambition of determination to move forward with accelerated success to devour the whole earth with its ancient yet in more recent times radical new age political views, leading the way in the creation of a complicated state of the art technologically advanced civilization. In the King James Version of the same scripture (Daniel 7:4) a man's heart was given to it. The definition of heart:** ***the primary organ of the blood's motion; the inner vital, or most essential part; seat of the affections, will; disposition of mind; conscience; courage; spirit; what represents a heart*****. The definition of disposition:** ***act of disposing; state of being disposed; arrangement; natural fitness; frame of mind; inclination*****. Do you see where it is leading an inclination a bias deviation or wandering from a normal direction of spiritual thinking.**

Which leads to the third and final scripture of Daniel 7:4 (New International Version) the word "torn" is used. The definition of torn: ***tear; split; ripped; severed; lacerated; broken; divided; impaired; damaged;***

spoiled; ruined. **The definition of tear:** ***to be torn; to pull with force; split; divide with doubt; to disrupt; to wreck; tear down; to dismantle.*** **The definition of ruined:** ***to fall; destroyed; downfall; bring to ruin; overthrow; subverted; desolate; dissolved; defaced; reduced.*** **The give and take scenario described from the plucked, pulled or tearing of the wings to a man's mind and or heart given is simply "change" an ever continual fact of history. The definition of change:** ***to put or take in place of something else; to alter; to exchange; to make different; vary.*** **The definition of vary:** ***to deviate or depart from.***

The West social and political atmosphere bringing about an evolution of change with such deviate subverted thinking shall from within their own hidden agenda slowly dissolve or dismantle by design the Democratic processes of God given freedom and liberty in exchange to pursue of their own whole hearted and opened minded self-interests of ingenuity and material progress. Causing the West to lift up or arise from the dark ages to a new age of intellectual enlightenment and reasoning as the independent dominating world powers. The consequences of their actions however has created a spiritual downfall of needless suffering, division and restless Godless disorder concluding the wise and knowledgeable Western powers stand alone in their desolate spiritual ruin. There is a saying: "Therefore in the absence of truth our love is misguided and is nothing but a perversion if we hear but reject truth. Then we are revealed as goats." From the beginning history has proven once man has turn from the truth leaving the presence of God and ventured out in search of his own self-relying knowledge instead of faith all around disaster was never far away. Today departing from the everlasting truth of God and choosing to live

on his own terms man's love has become perverted and twisted. In exchange for their love of God many choose to pursue the love of their own self-interests and the many material things the world has to offer. Living in empty miserable denial of God the West aware of their spiritual and moral decline is now in a condemned state of forsaken rejection by examination from the Lord.

The wings plucked, pulled or torn off and a man's mind and or heart given did not take place overnight. It was a gradual simultaneous process that took generations of time. The western alliance mind and heart were set upon a course towards the creation of a more prosperous and self-sufficient future. This "change" in the heart and mind caused a slow gradual steadfast separation from God. Ambitious thinking in a bright promising future was in a routine manner handed down to each new generation and taught through many institutions of learning. And as technology materialized, this inspired the ambiguous thinking for more advancement and change. And the exciting new world of progress continued to lure more ideas of success into the hearts and minds of many around the globe creating an even more widening gap of separation from God to the point of no return. Adding insult to injury mankind proud without shame of his achievements with the ever increasing knowledge continues a practice through his art and science to mock and even question the very existence of God. As a result the satanic inspired power is now out of control corrupting and transforming the entire social and political face of the earth into a restless worldwide Apostate Church readying and preparing to receive the Antichrist.

With the presence of the strengthening Bear and its growing numbers of allies, America has become consumed with fear and accelerated her efforts of technological advancements in order to protect the free world from foreign aggression speeding ahead the last days.

THE SECOND BEAST

Daniel 7:5 (Modern Translation) - "The second beast looked like a bear with its paw raised, ready to strike. It held three ribs between its teeth, and I heard a voice saying to it, "Get up! Devour many people." The Second Beast is the Russian Bear the greater and lesser of the superpowers. The Bear's paw raised and poised to strike is Russia taking a tactical offensive and defensive military stance that is ready, willing and able to unleash its huge military might at any threatening foe.

The three ribs between the Bear's teeth represent the three traditional western allies the United States, Canada and the United Kingdom. Why the rib? Genesis 2:23-24 (King James Version) - "And Adam said, This is now bone of my bones, and flesh of my flesh; she shall be called Woman, because she was taken out of Man. Therefore shall a man leave his father and his mother, and shall cleave unto his wife; and they shall be one flesh." In scripture, the rib is a word to express a link from the forefathers through to their descendants.

The three ribs between its teeth is also Russia's long standing political indifference with the free world. How so? The ribs are bones. The definition of bone:

a hard substance forming the framework of an animal. Ordinarily animals gnaw away at bare bones. The definition of gnaw: *to bite in agony or rage; to cause steady annoying pain.* It has been since the discovery of the new world the very presence of the Russian Bear had instantly become a growing steadfast gnawing and or annoying pain of fearful eastern policy posing many threats to the struggling free world's way of life, a permanent thorn in the side of generations of western descendants and or teeth gnawing on their rib bones. And to bring it all to a sudden end, the voice of evil's authority giving the command to the Russian Bear to attack and devour much flesh, unleashing the unthinkable a global thermal nuclear third world war.

The Third Beast

In the order of their appearance each beast is rising out of the troubled sea of nations to its state of authority. When the atomic bomb was successfully tested in the New Mexico desert on July 16, 1945 at 5:29:45 Am the United States officially became the world's first nuclear superpower. The nuclear supremacy had obviously added more bargaining muscle to the United States and the Western alliance. The next huge beast to arise is the Russian Bear. Russia became the second nuclear superpower on August 29, 1949. And now that history has allowed mankind to view the first two huge beasts. God's appointed time is quickly coming for the third huge beast to arise. When mankind has progressed as far as he is allowed to go, to prepare the world stage for fulfillment of God's end time prophecies. Then the third huge beast will arise from the troubled sea of nations.

Daniel 7:6 (King James Version) - "After this I beheld, and lo another, like a leopard, which had upon the back of it four wings of a fowl; the beast had also four heads; and dominion was given to it." The third huge beast is the Antichrist. The strange creature appears as a leopard. The leopard is a member of the cat family a carnivorous predator known for its tremendous speed, agility and hunting abilities. In Greek mythology the symbolic meaning of the leopard is a "hardy and determined warrior capable of overcoming by force and courage." As a matter of fact the reality of the Antichrist is just that, a hungry predator feared by many. The four wings represent several different truths about him. He is a bird of prey.

Ezekiel 38:8 (Modern Translation) - "A long time from now you will be called to action. In distant years you will swoop down onto the land of Israel."

Isaiah 46:11 (Modern Translation) - "I will call that swift bird of prey from the east - that man Cyrus from far away. And he will come and do my bidding. I have said I would do it and I will."

Jeremiah 49:22 (Modern Translation) - "The one who will come will fly as swift as a vulture and will spread his wings against Bozrah. Then the courage of the mightiest will disappear like that of a woman in labor."

The wings represent much more that a bird of prey. It is a double edge sword. The definition of four: ***twice two; three and one*****. The definition of fourfold:** ***quadruple*****. The definition of quadruple:** ***four times the sum or number*****. The definition of sum:** ***to recapitulate; to reckon up*****. The definition of recapitulate:** ***to repeat***

briefly. The reason for the four wings is simply a repeat of history. Antichrist had lived before (the first pair of wings) as a merciless king and warlord, feared throughout the ancient world. And he will rise from his own ashes of the past and live again (the second pair of wings).

Another meaning to the wings, the definition of wing: *flight; to fly.* The definition of flight: *lofty elevation; extravagant sally.* The definition of sally: *into public view; a dart of intellect; to leap forth.* The definition of extravagant: *lavish; wasteful; exceeding due bounds; fantastic.* The wings will bring him to a lofty elevation of lavishly extravagant earthly power before all mankind to witness. His throne of power and extravagant life style beyond man's reach will be short lived.

The definition of fantastic: *pertaining to fantasy or fancy; visionary; whimsical.* The definition of whim: *a sudden fancy; a caprice.* The definition of caprice: *a freak; a sudden or unreasonable change of opinion.* The definition of freak: *sudden causeless turn of the mind; to variegate.* The definition of variegate: *to diversify in appearance.* The definition of diversify: *to make diverse in form or qualities.* The definition of diverse: *different; unlike various.* The definition of divert: *to turn aside; to amuse; a feigned attack.* The definition of amuse: *to beguile.* The definition of beguile: *to practice guile on; to dupe.* The definition of guile: *fraud; duplicity.* The definition of duplicity: *doubleness of heart or speech; deception; to trick.* The definition of deceive: *to mislead the mind of; to impose on; to frustrate hopes.* The definition of impose: *to deceive; to victimize.* This last set of definitions show how the Antichrist will be a diverse and fraudulent man. A master of deception who will accomplish all he sets out to do. A clever

and misleading visionary appearing to have all the answers, he shall victimize many luring them away from God. And lead Antichrist to great heights of fear and honor. Once all the authority and power has been placed under his control, the Antichrist shall show his true colors of deception. The Beast shall change all morals and laws to enslave under his full control an unsuspecting world a spiritual assault frustrating hopes by promising mankind endless peace and plenty all the while plotting their destruction.

The four heads are four of the seven heads of the fourth huge beast. According to Revelation 17:10 (Modern Translation) - "They also represent seven kings. Five have already fallen, the sixth now reigns, the seventh is yet to come, but his reign will be brief." What all this means is that in Daniel's time, history was up to four of the seven heads or kings. When John wrote the book of Revelation, history was up to the sixth head or king. And the seventh was yet to come. It goes on in Revelation 17:11 (Modern Translation) - "The scarlet animal that died is the eighth king having reign before as one of the seven; after his second reign, he too will go to his doom." Another description of this eighth king Antichrist coming to life again is Revelation 13:3 (Modern Translation) - "I saw that one of his heads seemed wounded beyond recovery but the fatal wound was healed! All the world marveled at this miracle and followed the Creature in awe."

The final description of the third huge beast is that dominion or sovereign authority was given to it over all mankind. Revelation 13:2 (Modern Translation) - "This Creature looked like a leopard but had bear's feet and a lion's mouth! And the Dragon gave him his own power and throne and great authority." Under God's prophetic supervision, Satan The Dragon has

chosen one king. This king is Satan's chosen son the Antichrist an angry fiend who "reflects the presence and influence of Satan within him." In other words a powerful king in which Satan's dark spirit will live and work his evil and destined will. A mysterious king from the past that shall soon rise from the pit of hell and live again to inherit the power and throne and great authority to rule over all mankind.

THE FOURTH BEAST

Daniel 7:7 (Modern Translation) - "Then, as I watched in my dream, a fourth animal rose up out of the ocean, too dreadful to describe and incredibly strong. It devoured some of its victims by tearing them apart with its huge iron teeth, and others it crushed beneath its feet. It was far more brutal and vicious than any of the other animals, and it had ten horns."

Daniel 7:23-24 (King James Version) - "Thus he said, "The fourth beast shall be the fourth kingdom upon the earth, which shall be diverse from all kingdoms, and shall devour the whole earth, and shall tread it down, and break it into pieces. And the ten horns out of this kingdom are ten kings that shall arise; and another shall rise after them; and he shall be diverse from the first, and he shall subdue three kings."

Revelation 13:1-2 (Modern Translation) - "And now, in my vision, I saw a Strange Creature rising up out of the sea. It had seven heads and ten horns, and ten crowns upon its horns. And written on each head were blasphemous names, each one defying and insulting God. This Creature looked like a leopard but had

bear's feet and a lion's mouth! And the Dragon gave him his own power and throne and great authority."

Revelation 17:3-4 (Modern Translation) - "So the angel took me in spirit into the wilderness. There I saw a woman sitting on a scarlet animal that had seven heads and ten horns, written all over with blasphemies against God. The woman wore purple and scarlet clothing and beautiful jewelry made of gold and precious gems and pearls, and held in her hand a golden goblet full of obscenities."

The vision of the Strange Creature John witnessed and recorded in Revelation 13:1-2 is identical to the Four Wild Beasts (united) of Daniel's dream. The Fourth Beast, odd in its appearance exhibits its own anomalies.

Far more complicated than first realized the Fourth Wild Beast represents a chain of events in the past, present and future rolled into one symbolic illustration. With the rise of each beast and the momentous sequence of events surrounding their individual creation the Fourth Wild Beast gradually begins to take form. And as the birth of their union takes place the Strange Fourth Wild Beast is rising from the troubled and restless sea of nations.

The Fourth Beast is a diverse kingdom created first by the Eastern and Western powers (the first two beasts). These modern industrialized nations shall mutually agree to an armistice to prevent all-out war between the two opposing sides. The leaders in their hopes would graft the East and West together (as to mix iron with clay) to try and heal the wounds of the past. This in fact is the "New World Order" or NWO. A revolutionary new system devouring the whole earth

stomping out the present world order and breaking it into pieces treading down any rogue nation, group or individual on either side who attempts to sabotage the process. Force by example to crush any and all threats that may weaken the alliance. Visible actions of punishment to insure one side will not suspect the other of plotting any kind of military and or political takeover of the other. Reviving cold war tensions (including another arms race) to a worse state than it originally began. To keep a long complicated story short: the Eastern and Western powers announce a formal truce shaping and creating a NWO a cease fire giving birth to a possible worldwide declaration of martial law. Too crush any uprisings threatening to disrupt any official proceedings leading to a one world government.

The meaning of Daniel 7:7, I have learned is horrible to say the least. This scripture in all its reality is revealing many resisting the NWO inevitably leading to armed confrontations with law enforcement officials and even the military causing untold numbers of casualties worldwide. Scarring the living for life in many tragic ways children permanently separated from parents one heartbreaking story after another. This is the eye opening translation the Lord revealed to me of the Fourth Huge Beast as it tears its victims apart with its huge iron teeth and devours them in combat. Crushing or to overpower and oppress others beneath its feet with its stern procedures of martial law. My advice concerning this particular coming prophecy is do not under any circumstances allow these unseen enemy forces bait you into a hopeless cause taking up arms against the authorities. To fight the NWO is to fight against God's prophecies, and God shall allow your enemies to conquer and punish you. Matthew

26:52 (King James Version) - "Then said Jesus unto him. Put up again thy sword into his place; for all they that take the sword shall perish with the sword." The translation is taking up not just the sword a physical weapon. It is also the physiological weapon of warfare of hate and revenge. Which grafted together creates a deadly combination. Not only may you lose your life in any armed resistance, you may lose your soul to the deceiving powers of the underworld an enormous amount of harm for all concerned.

The scripture of Daniel 7:23-24 reveals more detail of the next sequence of events to come. Out of the Fourth Wild Beast or NWO shall arise the ten horns or ten kings to their positions of authority, and following the ten kings, another king shall arise a diverse brutal king: Antichrist (the third beast). They shall form an alliance together fulfilling the prophecy Revelation 17:3-4 and creating the Scarlet Animal with seven heads and ten horns. The alliance is placing the finishing touches upon the Fourth Wild Beast causing this horrifying Strange Wild Creature to rise from the troubled sea of nations in full view.

Revelation 17:16-17 (Modern Translation) - "The Scarlet Animal and his ten horns - which represent ten kings who will reign with him - all hate the woman, and will attack her and leave her naked and ravaged by fire. For God will put a plan into their minds, a plan that will carry out his purposes: They will mutually agree to give their authority to the scarlet animal, so that the words of God will be fulfilled." The plan: Attack the modern woman America with the dreaded third world war to overthrow her worldwide throne and subdue three kings of the western alliance the United States, Canada and the United Kingdom.

The definition of subdue: *to subjugate; to overpower; to tame; to soften; to tone down.* The definition of subjugate: *to subdue; to conquer and compel; to submit.* These two words may be performed in different ways and yet have the same basic fundamental meaning.

The word subdue may be used to win an argument of controversy between two individuals or two nations. And the same can be said of an armed confrontation. Antichrist without hesitation may use both with his master plan for world domination. While certain nations shall face total annihilation, the fate of others is to be overpowered and beaten into repentance. Still others only tamed to serve as trusted allies. The whole earth will be subdued in one form or another.

Daniel 7:8 (Modern Translation) - "As I was looking at the horns, suddenly another small horn appeared among them, and three of the first ones were yanked out, roots and all, to give it room; this little horn had a man's eyes and a bragging mouth." The next two scriptures reveal further detail. The small horn with man's eyes and a bragging mouth is the Antichrist and his rise to power. He (Antichrist) is to subdue and or uproot the first three and as common sense dictates the first three to be the three traditional allies the United States, Canada and the United Kingdom. The basic architects of the modern world the three allies subdued and uprooted by force from the world scene to make room for the new headmaster, Antichrist.

Revelation 13:11-12 (Modern Translation) - "Then I saw another strange animal, this one coming up out of the earth, with two little horns like a lamb but a fearsome voice like the Dragon's. He exercised all

the authority of the Creature whose death-wound had been healed, whom he required all the world to worship." The definition of two: ***one and one together.*** **The definition of one:** ***closely united; union or concord.*** **The definition of concord:** ***union in feelings or opinions; harmony; agreements of words in construction.*** **The definition of union:** ***act of joining; combination; agreement; harmony; marriage; confederacy; league; an alliance.*** **The definition of horn:** ***a hard projection on the heads of certain animals.*** **The definition of projection:** ***act of projecting; a prominence.*** **The definition of projector:** ***one who plans.*** **The definition of prominence:** ***state of being prominent; projection; protuberance.*** **The definition of prominent:** ***eminent.*** **The definition of eminent:** ***exalted; high in office; distinguished; illustrious.*** **The definition of illustrious:** ***re-owned; celebrated; noble; conferring honor or glorious.*** **The definition of noble:** ***lofty in character; magnificent; a person of rank; a peer.*** **The definition of re-owned:** ***famous; celebrated; remarkable; eminent.*** **This particular scripture reveals few details of this other strange creature with two little horns and the Dragon's voice rising from the earth and or grave of hell. However, even with the few descriptions the creature appears as what is now known as the Unholy Trinity. The strange creature with the Dragon's voice is Satan. The two little horns like a lamb is the Antichrist and his False Prophet. The definition of lamb:** ***the young of the sheep.*** **The young to Satan's ancient lifespan the False Prophet is an assistant and noble peer in alliance with the Antichrist Revelation 19:20. The two little horns have joined and become one united in spirit under Satan's power. Satan's most prized and trusted servants. Three separate entities, and yet who work in one mind, heart, body and spirit.**

Preceding and immediately following the third world war overthrow Satan himself exercise all authority through the Antichrist and the False Prophet. At that point in history the Unholy Trinity Revelation 16:13 is in their absolute complete pinnacle of power. The Unholy Trinity: Satan (the Dragon), Antichrist (the false Messiah), the False Prophet (the unholy spirit who exercise all commands of the Antichrist). The False Prophet is a true angel of death an enforcer who harshly nurtures and practices deceiving tactics of fear to gain worldwide control and obedience to the Beast-Antichrist radical new changes of international law.

Do not be confused over the symbolic meanings. Purposely it is a closed door of mystery meant to conceal the truth of God's future prophecies. Why, simply because man would try to alter the future for his own benefit working against the eternal will of God. Nevertheless, the key to unlock and understand these future events is prayer. Viewing the Antichrist as the Scarlet Beast of a man and a Leopard predator of war or even a bird of prey among other descriptions given to him over time, is revealing who he is from different points of view. As reading and turning the pages in a book the more pages you turn and read, the more detail to the mystery is uncovered and by connecting the dots the clearer the picture of understanding. We in this generation who live in the age of information are very fortunate to be allowed to learn and witness for ourselves the last days. It has become my own personal experience the closer man approaches to the fulfillment of these prophecies the more is naturally revealed, aiding in the advancement of prophetic knowledge and the guiding wisdom of understanding.

To give a brief summary of the Fourth Wild Beast and the events leading to its creation: Somewhere

amidst the vast oasis of world peace mingled with conflict of the NWO between the East and West (the first two Beasts). Antichrist (immediately following the ten horns seated in their states of power) at the appropriate time frame ascends from hell to fulfill his destiny. Antichrist - The Third Beast Daniel 7:6 or little horn Daniel 7:8 working in stealth shall confer with ten previously selected kings (the ten horns). And God will reveal a plan into their minds carrying out his will. To subdue the first three nations or kingdoms responsible for the creation of the new modern technological world empire the three traditional allies who reign as the world's influential heads of state the United States, Canada and the United Kingdom. Antichrist and his ten horn or ten king alliance shall attack and subdue the traditional western allies with the dreaded third world war and overcome and or uproot them. To overthrow by force the modern woman America's worldly throne of leadership. And strip her of all wealth and power and to sabotage and divert mankind course toward world peace and establish Satan's one world government. Antichrist, victorious rules from his satanic inspired throne built upon the ashes of the west. He shall stand unchallenged. Satan the Dragon exercises all authority through his two servants: Antichrist and his False Prophet. Wearing down the peoples of the world with persecution and to change all morals and laws throughout the world and subdue and or punish anyone who challenges Antichrist's authority. Deceiving and or encouraging all the nations to leave their beliefs and follow him. He (Antichrist) shall succeed in everything he sets out to do, subduing the inhabitants of the earth under far deeper suppression and or submission than the NWO. The nations sinking from one level of darkness (NWO), to the next (under

Satan's one world government) too try as they may (unsuccessfully) to extinguish the illuminating eternal life of truth from the earth until the nations remain in complete total spiritual darkness.

Beware the NWO is a crystal clear sign. Remain vigilant. The moment this formal peace agreement takes place between the East and the West man shall walk through the doorway to the age of the Antichrist. Prepare, the season of these significant events is drawing close.

The Ram and the Goat

Daniel 8:17 (Modern Translation) - "So Gabriel started toward me. But as he approached, I was too frightened to stand, and fell down with my face to the ground. "Son of man," he said, "you must understand that the events you have seen in your vision will not take place until the end times come." The first year of King Belshazzar's reign over the Babylonian Empire Daniel received the dream of the Four Mighty Beasts. The third year of King Belshazzar's reign Daniel received a distinct vision in relation to the Four Wild Beasts. Daniel at Susa, the capital in the Province Elam, stood beside the Ulai River. What Daniel witnessed was an extraordinary scene.

Daniel 8:3-12 (King James Version) - "Then I lifted up mine eyes, and saw, and behold, there stood before the river a Ram which had two horns; and the two horns were high; but one was higher than the other, and the higher came up last. I saw the Ram pushing westward, and northward, and southward; so that no beasts might stand before him, neither was there any

that could deliver out of his hand; but he did according to his will, and became great. And as I was considering, behold He Goat came from the west on the face of the whole earth, and touched not the ground; and the Goat had a notable horn between his eyes. And he came to the Ram that had two horns, which I had seen standing before the river, and ran unto him in the fury of his power. And I saw him come close unto the Ram, and he was moved with choler against him, and smote the Ram, and broke his two horns; and there was no power in the Ram to stand before him, but he cast him down to the ground, and stamped upon him; and there was none that could deliver the Ram out of his hand. Therefore the he goat waxed very great; and when he was strong; the great horn was broken; and for it came up four notable ones toward the four winds of heaven. And out of one of them came forth a little horn, which waxed exceeding great, toward the south, and toward the east, and toward the pleasant land. And it waxed great, even to the host of heaven; and it cast down some of the host and of the stars to the ground, and stamped upon them. Yea, he magnified himself even the prince of the host, and by him the daily sacrifice was taken away, and the place of his sanctuary was cast down. And a host was given him against the daily sacrifice by reason of transgression, and it cast down the truth to the ground; and it practiced and prospered."

Daniel 8:3-12 (Modern Translation) - "As I was looking around, I saw a ram with two long horns standing on the river bank, and as I watched, one of these horns began to grow, so that it was longer than the other. The ram butted everything out of its way and no one could stand against it or help its victims. It did as it pleased and became very great. While I was wondering what

this could mean, suddenly a buck goat appeared from the west, so swiftly that it didn't even touch the ground. This goat, which had one very large horn between its eyes, rushed furiously at the two-horned ram. And the closer he came, the angrier he was. He charged into the ram and broke off both his horns. Now the ram was helpless and the buck goat knocked him down and trampled him, for there was no one to rescue him." The victor became both proud and powerful, but suddenly, at the height of his power, his horn was broken, and in its place grew four good-sized horns pointing in four directions. One of these, growing slowly at first, soon became very strong and attacked the south and east, and warred against the land of Israel. He fought against the people of God and defeated some of their leaders. He even challenged the Commander of the army of heaven by canceling the daily sacrifices offered to him, and by defiling his Temple. But the army of heaven was restrained from destroying him for this transgression. As a result, truth and righteousness perished, and evil triumphed and prospered."

Daniel 8:3-12 (New International Version) - "I looked up, and there before me was a ram with two horns, standing beside the canal, and the horns were long. One of the horns was longer than the other but grew up later. I watched the ram as it charged toward the west and the north and the south. No animal could stand against it, and none could rescue from its power. It did as it pleased and became great. As I was thinking about this, suddenly a goat with a prominent horn between its eyes came from the west, crossing the whole earth without touching the ground. It came toward the two-horned ram I had seen standing beside the canal and charged at it in great rage. I saw it attack the ram

furiously, striking the ram and shattering its two horns. The ram was powerless to stand against it; the goat knocked it to the ground and trampled on it, and none could rescue the ram from its power. The goat became very great, but at the height of its power the large horn was broken off, and in its place four prominent horns grew up toward the four winds of heaven. Out of one of them came another horn, which started small but grew in power to the south and to the east and toward the Beautiful Land. It grew until it reached the host of the heavens, and it threw some of the starry host down to the earth and trampled on them. It set itself up to be as great as the commander of the army of the Lord; it took away the daily sacrifice from the Lord, and his sanctuary was thrown down. Because of rebellion, the Lord's people and the daily sacrifice were given over to it. It prospered in everything it did, and truth was thrown to the ground."

THE RAM

The Ram is the fifth Beast of Daniel's unique prophetic book written with heavens inspired knowledge and wisdom hidden behind the locked door of many symbolic meanings. The Ram the sheep and the Goat are all from the same family totem. The Ram with its aggressive strength is a symbol of, authority and ruler-ship, the male of the sheep is very territorial in nature protecting the herd and is bothered when others violate their space. The Ram is also a creature which signifies sacrifice Genesis 22:13. In the book of Numbers it lists several scriptures one use for the Ram was a "fellowship offering" sacrifice to the Lord. The definition of fellow: ***a partner; a companion; one of the***

same kind. **The definition of fellowship:** ***companionship; joint interest; an association.***

The horn is a biblical description symbolized by tremendous power, dominion, glory, victory and success, simply the larger the horn, greater the success. As all horns have in common there also means of attack and defense strength and honor, the Ram with the two large separate horns the larger horn rising up last reveals one king and his empire outgrowing the other. The separation of the two horns reveals the division between the Medes (the smaller horn) ruled by King Astyages (King of the Median Empire from 585 – 550 BC) who conquered and liberated by the Persians (Persia the ancient name for modern day Iran - the larger horn) ruled by King Cyrus the Great II (reigning King and founder of the Persian Empire from 559 – 530 BC). According to history in 550 BC the Persian King Cyrus the Great revolted against his grandfather King Astyages and in a fierce struggle as history was written (even though some dates may vary) victorious over the Median Empire (also of Modern Iran) in about 550 to 549 BC. In a domino effect the entire empire coalition of the Lydian Empire (Modern Turkey) fell in 546 BC, and Neo Babylonian Empire (modern Iraq and Syria) fell in 539 BC and were brought under total submission and liberation creating the ever expanding Persian Empire. At its peak the Persian Empire under Darius I the Great (522 – 486 BC) extended from the Balkans in Europe and Egypt in North Africa to India in Central Asia. However it was not the enormous size of the Persian Empire which was impressive it was what King Cyrus accomplished which was not only extraordinary it was revolutionary for his time. He appeared not the conqueror, but a liberator a merciful diplomatic ruler who allowed all under his leadership

their freedom and with respect to his fellow citizens the continued practice of their customs and religions. King Cyrus also freed the Jews from Babylonian slavery and granted permission for them to return and rebuild their homeland including Solomon's Temple. Earning him the honorable title King Cyrus the Great. "The Persian Empire under the rule of King Cyrus the Great were humane in their governance which in turn gave birth to the first laws of human rights."

Asia is the emergence of civilization to include the birthplace of major religions known. These religions have lived with one another for thousands of years and have been the cradle of the human race. Moving from the East toward the West, South and North the Ram represents the ancient Persian Empire. The origins of the first civilization and creator of the first human rights declaration with worldwide descendants (of many races and nationalities) who have been influenced, guided and protected by their leaders, have continued the practice of all their ancient traditions for generations without any interference appears unstoppable while advancing across the earth. And the Ram shall clash head on against the Goat who not only represents ancient Greece also in future tense represents the western new intellectual age of progress and enlightenment.

The Ram is stopped dead in it tracks as the Goat tramples out all the "ruling" ancient traditions and practices attempting a fellowship offering of sacrifice to create a peaceful new worldwide civilization with all sides in a joint interest involving law and order/ modern human rights policies establishing a peaceful acceptance between the ancient traditional practices of faith and the modern new age of science and progress. People everywhere in the cultivation and evolution of

their thinking shall gradually over time mistakenly sacrifice all their own traditional values and personal religious faith in pursuit of a more modern and attractive luxurious life style of wealth, privilege and prestige. Ruining their very own spiritual life, and revealing their independent thinking of the Goat.

THE GOAT

"Classical Greece is generally considered to be the seminal culture which provided the Foundation of Western Civilization"

The Goat is a particular beast in the biblical descriptions coinciding with its actions. One must first begin to learn this unique creature's nature. Its natural habits reveal a common pattern of thinking. According to astrologers the symbolic meaning of the Goat (and the Ram) possesses an abundance of knowledge, myth and lore. "Goats are not communal often they spread themselves apart grazing alone. With a sense of independence they respect distance and space. They also encourage independent adventures and explorations of high vistas for the sole purpose of gaining individual knowledge. Goats love to climb heights, traveling and living with ease and enthusiasm at impossible angles and elevations which reveals a strong will of desire for progress and achievement. With a determined and strong free spirit mingled in curiosity and inquiry of personal ambition. Expressing discrimination and a willingness to explore and hold out for what is desired. Alistair Cooke once wrote: "Curiosity is often a sign of free-wheeling intelligence." Curiosity and intelligence

go hand in hand. The Goat is a grand reminder of this and urges to be inquisitive."

As the Europeans sailed westward to the new blessed island North America, colonies sprang up and down the eastern seaboard. Overtime the English rule created a heavy yoke of oppression over the British colonies in which small bands of militia struggled to gain popular support from a weary hesitant over taxed population. Eventually the oppression turned to frustration which began to create an atmosphere of revolt. Angry organized and disorganized protests began to surface causing the unforgettable Boston Massacre on March 5, 1770 with the killing and injuring of several civilians by British soldiers sent to the city to maintain law and order. And to insure paying their more than fair share of taxes to the Kingdom of Great Britain for example through the Townshend Revenue Acts of 1767 (named after Chancellor of Exchequer which is equivalent to the Secretary of the Treasury in America today Charles Townshend August 27, 1725 – September 4, 1767 who before his death drafted a series of organized acts of taxation passed by the Parliament of Great Britain upon United Kingdom's imported goods arriving into the British colonies of North America) or the Boston tea party on the night of December 16, 1773 both incidents in defiance of several struggling imposed and repealed Acts (a taxation to raise money to pay for the standing armies and other British authority figures of power in North America at the time, an over taxed and lagging English economy due to the ever growing war debt from the French and Indian war between Britain and France 1754 - 1763) began to reveal their displeasure towards the royal throne. Which eventually lead to armed confrontations between British soldiers and the colonist militia of the first known battle at the town of Lexington Massachusetts April 19, 1775. Titled: "The shot heard round the world." The tense standoff at the town of Lexington on the early morning of April 19th between approximately seventy half sober Massachusetts colonial Militia commanded by Captain John Parker (July 13, 1729 – September 17, 1775 also a farmer and mechanic who died not in combat, of tuberculosis ordered: "Stand your ground, don't fire unless fired upon, but if they mean to have war let it begin here" Paul Revere recalled Parker ordering: "Do not molest them without they begin first") and a total fighting force of seven hundred exhausted British regulars commanded by Lieutenant Colonel Francis Smith (1723 – 1791). At point commanding a detachment force of two hundred British light Infantry was Major John Pitcairn (December 28, 1722 – June 17, 1775 – Pitcairn was shot and severely wounded as he and his British Marines were charging American held positions at the battle of Bunker Hill and later died in Boston and buried in the Old North Church) who had been maneuvering secretly in the cover of night to recover war materials (rumored hidden in the town of Concord to the northwest of Lexington). The red coats were also ordered to arrest Samuel Adams (September 27, 1722 – October 2, 1803) and John Hancock (January 23, 1737 – October 8, 1793) for treason. The two men both open critics of English occupation and Adams a financier of the growing rebellion to British rule were staying in Lexington at the Hancock-Clarke house. Once arriving near the town of Lexington Major Pitcairn found the colonist (warned by Paul Revere January 1, 1735 – May 10 1818 a silversmith and engraver – an early

industrialist and patriot who bear witness to the battles at Lexington and Concord) standing at the ready and ordered the militia to throw down their arms and disperse. At first the militia held their ground Captain Parker ordered his men to go home but retain their muskets and after a few tense moments they began to murmur between themselves and began to slowly break ranks and walk away carrying their weapons. Reports on what happened in the brief battle at Lexington are confused and contradictory. Nevertheless here is where it gets interesting. Without warning one then several more shots were fired and history has failed to reveal the hidden details as to who or why? From which direction the shots came to this day remains a mystery. Once hearing the shots the anxious British soldiers (who knew they were marching through enemy held territory) responded by firing on the colonist militia. By then the militia in their hasty retreat began to lock, load and return fire. The British responded once again and charged with fixed bayonets sending the militia scattering in their retreat. Major Pitcairn ordered a cease fire when the smoke cleared the engagement left approximately seven to eight colonists dead and nine wounded. With one British soldier wounded in the thigh and Major John Pitcairn's horse had been hit at least two times (as if the excited militia were aiming for the major). When Lieutenant Colonel Francis Smith arrived with reinforcements he ordered his nerves men to regroup and moved on to the town of Concord as ordered (the British's primary mission ordered by Royal Military Governor British General Thomas Gage 1719 – 1787) which eventually lead to the decisive battle at the (as it is named today) Old North Bridge outside of the town of Concord was guarded by a detachment force

of ninety to one hundred red coats from the 4th, 10th, and 43rd Regiments in which one-third lay dead or wounded in a confrontation of regrouping colonists (at the start who witnessed for themselves from a distance on a nearby hill to the old north bridge the British in the town of Concord burning war materials and accidently a building caught fire which the colonialist believed the British were burning the town of Concord down) were consisting of approximately (the reports on the numbers of men vary) several companies of minutemen, and several companies of Massachusetts militia along with others from neither group totaling nearly four hundred men. The incident at Lexington sent shockwaves of anger and protest throughout the thirteen colonies. And the rest as they say is history. Historians may disagree the battle at Lexington where the small seeds sown which gave birth to the greatest most powerful nation the world has ever seen the United States of America.

The point to the brief history lesson is the conclusive battle at Lexington Massachusetts eventually lead to a war for Independence and is to this day a continuing revolution renewing the engine of progress and innovation through the philosophy of logical thought and reason. The American Empire, a new order of the ages. The unveiling was not only with military weapons of war but with great state papers set in place forged by the founding fathers. And as the population increased many seeking more open living space began their expansion westward headed by official expeditions such as Lewis and Clark.

The Lewis and Clark expedition or Corps of Discovery Expedition (May 1804 – September 1806) was headed by Captain Meriwether Lewis (August 18, 1774 – October 11, 1809) and Second Lieutenant

William Clark (August 1, 1770 – September 1, 1838). The expedition was commissioned by President Thomas Jefferson (April 13, 1743 – July 4, 1826) following the Louisiana Purchase of 1803. Overtime this spirit of adventure inspired the abundance of U.S. conquest and personal explorations from the military to mountain men to settlers continued the American expansion from the Mississippi river to the Continental divide to the Pacific coast leading to other surveys, purchases personal gains and expeditions brewing hatreds creating conflicts and historic battles taking place with native peoples in which thousands on both sides suffered and died.

The American way of thinking was then and is today shaped and cultivated into the mindset of the Goat described in myth and lore. I believe the surroundings of one's personal environment may create a powerful influence in the shaping of an individual's thinking. From the beginning historical events mingled with the final decisions of national policy makers have gradually over time cultivated and shaped the minds of the American people and their neighboring western nations. With the geographical location of North and South America, the signing of many great state papers declaring and constituting independence for all mankind through Western political and military wars of liberation and change; education and scientific breakthroughs and explorations into all fields has and is today benefited and accelerated mankind's efforts of success. Nevertheless walking hand in hand with the historical events I foresee the obvious breeding of many sins created by man's shallow faith and short-sighted understanding. The separation of church and state and the optional removal of prayer from the public schools, abortions, corruption and cover-ups

along with all other manner of sin running rampant everywhere one turns spreading and racing across the entire globe creating and displaying the same nature and thinking as the Goat – distinct and separate from the Lord our God.

The mindset of such thinking originated from Satan. Isaiah 14:12-17 (Modern Translation) – "How you are fallen from heaven O Lucifer, son of the morning! How you are cut down to the ground-mighty though you were against the nations of the world. For you said to yourself "I will ascend to heaven and rule the angels. I will take the highest throne. I will preside on the Mount of Assembly far away in the north. I will climb to the highest heavens and be like the Most High." But instead, you will be brought down to the pit of hell, down to its lowest depths. Everyone there will stare at you and ask, "Can this be the one who shook the earth and the kingdoms of the world? Can this be the one who destroyed the world and made it into a shambles and demolished its greatest cities and had no mercy on his prisoners?" Satan the fallen angel worshipped by many today broke ranks and separated himself from the family of God and desired to be the most high. The Dragon's followers display the very type of mentality. Through the very thoughts they reveal their works of art and literature. For example, the English occultist Edward Alexander Crowley (October 12, 1875 – December 1, 1947) aka Aleister Crowley wrote his famous book: "The Book of the Law" outlines the principles of his philosophy Thelema (Greek word meaning "will" or "intention"). The basic law of Thelema: "Do what thou wilt, shall be the whole of the law; love is the law, love under will" a religion of total self-expression. Another example is Alphonse Louis Constant (February 8, 1810 – May

31, 1875) aka Eliphas Levi was a French occult author and ceremonial magician. His drawing in 1865 of the pagan idol the Sabbatical Goat (later associated with Baphomet) was released. The name Baphomet (rumored was worshipped by the Knights Templar) and the portrait of the Sabbatical Goat combined has been connected with Satanism due to the adoption of the two by the church of Satan. The Sabbatical Goat represents the total sum of the universe. It portrays man and woman, day and night, good and evil, with the head or (thinking) of the Goat.

The Goat the sixth and final creature from the book of Daniel is a fearless creature with a large prominent horn between the eyes appearing from the West (inspired by the Western powers) crossing the whole earth with such tremendous speed it never touches the ground. The definition of height: *elevation; prominence; loftiness; to improve; to bring to a higher position; to promote; to make or become larger; greater; increase; strengthen; to improve; magnify*. The definition of speed: *swiftness; activity; eagerness; haste; hurry; readiness; agility; liveliness; expedition; alacrity; to help to succeed; aid fully informed; to prosper*. The definition of promote: *to advance; to encourage; to exalt; to raise to a higher position or rank; to further the growth; profit; develop; support; cultivate; improve; nourish; nurture; befriend; mentor; benefit; expand; better improve; cooperate; to subsidize*. The large horn between the eyes of the Goat is according to biblical scholars a symbol of great power. Even more symbolic evidence to the fact is the height at which the Goat swiftly moves above the ground is of great prospering and promoting heights of successfully developing power. The eyes it has been said are the windows of the soul (Matthew 6:22). The Goat eventually reveals through each visible beneficial

plan of action its insight, common sight and foresight of thought. The large protruding horn from between the eyes and or forehead of thinking was constructed and organized by design (inspired by the swift, proud and powerful Western powers) of highly intelligent men and women of vision.

As the Goat charged into the Ram it disintegrated the two horns of its power with brilliant planning. Knocking the Ram to the ground the Goat angry with determination using all vital tools at its deposal working in co-ordination at one solid goal attribute the forceful actions to create the earth moving change to trample or stomp out and abolish any and all resistance to the NWO. With standing power enough to completely reinvent and maintain under the continued United Nations law and order of controlled protection the political face and policy of thinking (to the mindset of the Goat) within the radical new ways of life throughout the whole earth to begin a new universal age of intellectual enlightenment.

At the victorious peek of its power the Goat at the precise time of history chosen the power of the large horn was broken or dismantled by design and four prominent horns with the four equal in political and military power extending into all four corners of the earth. In other words (as the Goat and its nature of thinking continues to thrive and survive) the beginning of The New World Order, a global union involving every form of institution known to man under one governmental world rule.

Out of the four horns another horn began to grow in power. Slowly at first and his power became very strong. The smaller horn is the Antichrist rising from the NWO, with his arrival the Beast's power shall grow slowly at first because of the fact people

will not know what to think of him. In the King James Version of Daniel 8:9 "a little horn which waxed exceeding great, toward the south, and toward the east, and toward the pleasant land." The definition of toward: ***in the direction; pointing to; on the way to; approaching; in relation to; close to.*** **The definition of relation: (relationship)** ***connection; association; family connection.*** **The definition of relationship:** ***kinship; affinity; bond; nearness; alliance; relevance; contact.*** **The definition of affinity:** ***attraction based on affection; fondness; liking; closeness; likeness; resemblance.*** **As time moves on the Beast shall spiritually attack with deceit and gain a close connect association of friendship and trust with many people from the South and the East meaning his strongest following or alliance shall appear from the poor of Asia and Africa. In the King James Version of Daniel 8:9 is written "The Pleasant Land." In the New International Version of the same scripture is written "The Beautiful Land." Meaning the pleasant and beautiful holy land of Israel, and the Beast shall bring peace between the peoples of Israel and Eastern peoples. Which shall draw in many Christians into the political arena of peace winning the hearts and minds of many people from all the other Gentile religions around the world with his complex art of deception increasing his popularity and strengthening his political power (created with his defying nature) to the far reaches of heaven, causing a challenging friction of mistrust not only with the Lord, between the Beast-Antichrist and Israel's closest strategic allied partner the United States.**

Daniel 20-22 (New International Version) - "The two-horned ram that you saw represents the kings of Media and Persia. The shaggy goat is the king of Greece, and

the large horn between its eyes is the first king. The four horns that replaced the one that was broken off represent four kingdoms that will emerge from his nation but will not have the same power." It has been stated: "The very rudiment of western civilization deprived from ancient Greece." The rudiment or the very fundamental principles of western Democracy originated from ancient Greece. One fine example the military tactics and strategies once utilized through Alexander the Great III of Macedon (20/21 July 356 – 10/11 June 323 BC) on many of his campaigns used and studied to this day. Alexander is recognized as one of history's most successful commanders.

The symbolic Goat with its natural independent mindset of living is the modern western system (the present king) of Democracy in its consistent state of evolution and the king represents and symbolically reflects his kingdom. Ancient Greece is the father of western Democracy and Democracy (the first king) which has been handed down through time rules the day. In other words the rough shaggy haired Goat is an organized system of western philosophical thoughts and beliefs passed down through time (still under a rough and difficult experiment of evolution and perfection) alive and maintained in the hearts and minds of those who serve it. And through a mutual agreement of the NWO from Western compounding pressures and threats of war, world opinion, technological progress and the peaceful and attractive displays of modern living the peoples of the Eastern nations shall merge with the West to dismantle and or disintegrate Eastern and Western obstacles and differences of all types to reorganize and provide a better life for all peoples of whom shall by their

choice remain in their peaceful and faithful religions. However the spear shall pierce and the wound run deep. Everyday life through the NWO may improve, however forced change of thinking from foreign pressures in eastern domestic and eastern foreign policy may cause a lingering fear and or resentment to a gradual abolishment of sacred faith. And this shall not be acceptable to others.

According to known historical events there is no debating with Historians and Biblical Scholars relating to past events leading to the rise and fall of both the Persian and Greek Empires. The ancient rivalry between the nations of Asia Africa and the Anglo pre and Christian nations of Europe and the west with the Holy land of Israel between the two has in fact never ended. The struggle for control of the Holy Land has been and continues today to be the main focal point of interest and hostility. However what I have noticed is their combined feats and enriched ideals of knowledge and wisdom from both sides which have withstood the test of time for future generations. The birth of the first organized civilization, politics, Democracy, human rights, religion, philosophy, literature, science, arts, mathematics, architecture, irrigation and agriculture which in fact laid the very foundation of the modern world we know today. Instead of the two opposing sides going to war they shall compromise and work together with willing sacrifices made with each respecting the other. And it is these eventful manmade plans of hope paving the road of universal peace for the New World Order the Beast himself shall aid in mending together and then cunningly divert from its intended course.

THE CONNECTION

In myth and lore the Ram and Goat were often interchangeable. The definition of interchange: ***to change; as one with the other; to exchange; to reciprocate; mutual change; exchange; alternate succession.*** **The definition of exchange:** ***to change one thing for another; to commute; to bargain.*** **The definition of bargain:** ***a contract; a gainful transaction.*** **The definition of contract:** ***to draw together; to make a mutual agreement; bond.*** **The definition of agreement:** ***harmony; conformity; stipulation.*** **The definition of harmony:** ***the just adaptation of parts to each other; concord; peace and friendship.*** **The definition of concord:** ***union in feelings; opinions; agreements of words in construction.*** **The contract defined is a concordant mutual agreement of peace and friendship among all nations written into law with the blood of countless numbers. A geo-political bond revealed as the New World Order. A vision mankind has strived for since the first sword was drawn on the battle field.**

The Goat trampling upon the Ram is the present system coming to an end with an interchangeable commencement providing a doorway to a more advanced enlightened age created and enforced through western influence. A New World Order, were all nations must relinquish their sovereignty to provide a more safe and peaceful environment with limited rights and privileges in order to form a more perfect one world union.

In the modern translation of Daniel 8:7 the word "trampled" is used. The definition of trample: ***to tread on heavily; to tread down; to treat with pride or insult; to treat in contempt; to tread with force.*** **In the King James Version of the same scripture the word**

"stamped" is used. The definition of stamp: ***to strike the foot forcibly downward; to impress; a mark imprinted; an instrument for crushing or for making impressions.*** **Daniel 7:33 (King James Version) – "Thus he said, The fourth beast shall be the fourth kingdom upon earth, which shall be diverse from all kingdoms, and shall devour the whole earth and shall tread it down, and break it into pieces." The definition of tread:** ***to set the foot on the ground; to copulate; to trample; gait; to walk on in a formal manner.*** **The definition of gait:** ***walk; manner of walking or stepping; carriage.*** **The definition of carriage:** ***act of carry; that which carries; vehicle; conveyance.*** **The definition of conveyance:** ***act or means of conveying; a carriage; transfer; a deed which transfer property.*** **The definition of transfer:** ***to convey from one place or person to another; to make over; act of transferring; removal of a thing from one place or person to another; something transferred.*** **The definition of break:** ***to sever by fracture; to rend; to open; to tame; to dissolve any union; to decline in vigor; to tell with discretion; to interrupt.*** **With the biblical descriptions it is clearly visible the Goat not only mimicked the actions of the Fourth Wild Beast in Daniel 7:23. It reveals more detail to the mystery as to where the actions and decision making originated from. Racing across from the west and devouring, trampling and treading down the face of the whole earth (a global transfer of authority) and breaking the present global system (or present world order) into pieces with incredible and unimaginable impressions of power necessary to interrupt, tame and or dissolve any and all unions of resistance. H.G. Wells wrote in 1939: "Countless people will hate the New World Order and will die protesting against it."**

Jeremiah 50:23 (Modern Translation) - "How Babylon, the mightiest hammer in all the earth, lies broken and shattered. Desolate among the nations!" A hammer shapes and creates. America since the beginning has been working tirelessly to forge and shape global policy for a new world order of the ages. The creation of the NWO is allowing the western powers most of all the United States the necessary leverage to encourage and guide the nations towards universal peace and harmony. America is sitting upon the Fourth Wild Beast of Revelation 17:3-4 unwittingly guiding the Strange Creature in the direction chosen to fulfill its destiny.

With the birth of the NWO, many uprisings and confrontations will quickly follow. Reaching at a point where the bloodshed will become so intense the peoples of the earth who have bared witness to the dead and dying. Their homes, even entire neighborhoods bomb and destroyed clashing with U.N. military forces and other authority figures. Will in their anguish and desperation proclaim with one universal voice for an end to the chaotic fighting.

With the overflowing sense of vulnerability and dread existing in wandering people everywhere. Their hearts and minds once under the order of conditioning are now prepared and readied to receive anyone or anything bringing hope to a weary war torn world. The mixture of events is at the precise time an open invitation rolling out the red carpet for the Antichrist's grand entrance. Then without warning the Beast shall reveal himself in the form of a peace maker. Through desperation many shall view the Beast as Jesus the Savior to lead the nations away from their mad course. Others shall view him as the Prophet Mohammad. And

other forms of hopeful belief's people around the globe may have in their blinding grief and stricken state of mind to comfort them. The reality, he is the Antichrist preying on the unsuspecting world.

The Arrival

Daniel 9:27 (New International Version) - "He will confirm a covenant with many for one seven. In the middle of the seven he will put an end to sacrifice and offering. And at the temple he will set up an abomination that causes desolation, until the end that is decreed is poured out on him." With the appearance of this unusual spiritual being and his "wise" solutions to mankind's many problems. He the Beast Antichrist shall create and confirm a covenant or agreement to the satisfaction of many people the world over.

Personally speaking no other book in the Holy Bible has taken my interest more than the book of Daniel. Particularly the challenging scripture of Daniel 9:27. However, it was the word "Week" in print which was confusing. Outside of the traditional use of the King James Version and the Modern Translation I found in my search for answers the "New International Version" of the Holy Bible. Within the same scripture the word "Seven" was printed. To understand the meaning of the mysterious scripture I decided to begin with reviewing select words by definition. And to my amazement a clear message appeared.

The definition of will: *legal declaration of a person as to what is to be done after death with property; to determine by choice*. The definition of confirm: *to make firm or more firm; to establish; to make certain;*

***to administer the rite of confirmation*. The definition of covenant: *a contract; compact; a writing containing the terms of an agreement; to enter into a formal agreement; to stipulate; to grant by covenant*. The definition of compact: *closely united; to consolidate; to unite firmly; an agreement; a contract*. The definition of many: *forming or comprising a number; numerous; the great majority of people; the crowd; the same number of; a certain number indefinitely*. The definition of one: *being closely united; union; concord*. The definition of concord: *union in feelings; opinions; harmony; agreement of words in construction*. The Beast shall arrive to end the worldwide spread of war and violence of the acclaimed NWO. He shall aid in the confirmation of a legal declaration establishing a closely united contract of agreement settling the differences of a great majority of people at first. With the Antichrist's gradual crafty methods of peace many shall become closely united in concord or in agreement within feelings, opinions, and harmony. However, in the King James Version the Modern Translation and the New International Version one word stands out. And that word is: "many." The Beast Antichrist shall confirm "a covenant with many." Not all! There are those throughout the world who will not trust him. They shall see right through his lies. Brave out spoken souls such as these shall be marked for termination by the Beast.**

The definition of week: *the space of seven days; space from one Sunday to another*. The definition of seven: *one more than six*. To begin with man is presumed to be a sevenfold being. The number seven is the most sacred and divine of any number. "It has had a very profound influence of society, most religions around the globe. In Christianity there are seven virtues

and seven deadly sins. In Buddhism there are seven sacraments. In the religion of Islam there are seven heavens and seven gates to seven hells. The number seven permeates every aspect of almost every religion. Even in today's modern world our lives are run by the number seven. There is seven days of the week. Seven wonders of the ancient world, seven continents. Seven colors of the rainbow, even seven notes in the musical scale to name a few."

Ordinarily over time the search for the proper words and their definitions became successful and routine. However I have to admit the two words: "week" and "seven" mingled separately in the scripture of Daniel 9:27 were perplexing. Unable to find a satisfactory set of definitions, with prayer I began to review the book of Genesis for understanding. Genesis 2:2-3 (Modern Translation) – "So on the seventh day, having finished his task, God ceased from this work he had been doing, and God blessed the seventh day and declared it holy, because it was the day when he ceased this work of creation." In the book of Genesis on the seventh day God rested from his work and blessed that day. "A disengagement as the work of creation was finished." The final conclusion: number seven denotes divine completion.

There is an old saying: "The teacher appears when the student is ready." It is at the proper point in time (when their hearts and minds are conditioned and readied) the Beast shall appear to many as God the savior and proclaim "divine completion" with his Christ like return as he confirms a covenant or agreement of global peace with many willing people around the world for "one seven" or to unite as one people under the divine completion of his return. The Beast shall proclaim: "This is your day of rest, the

beginning of a golden age of universal peace, safety and security." What the Antichrist shall strive for is: "strength through unity, unity through faith." Global rest and peace shall be achieved (for a temporary time). And life shall move on with many basking in false security as they look forward to a bright more prosperous future.

Following the worldwide celebrations of a renewed peace and prosperity the planned rebuilding of the global infrastructure shall begin. Including the erection of religious temple mounts dedicated in his name. Through time many shall become overwhelmed with his presence, even to the point of joyful obsession. Quickly forgetting the traditions of the past many shall begin to end the daily routine sacrifices and offerings to God. For in their thinking many shall believe the Beast-Antichrist is God. And agree to anything he suggests, changes and or commands. In desperation the wealthy and middle class more than willing to save their families and fortunes. And the poor who shall be more than willing to escape the harsh appalling conditions they have had to endure. The Antichrist shall offer humanity a new revived hope. From east to west and from north to south, far and near "many" in their current state of mind shall be ready, willing and able in their hypnotic trance to surrender their mortal lives and even their very souls to follow this man and his illusions of global peace and security. Antichrist's pen is as mighty as his sword.

Daniel 8:23-24 (Modern Translation) - "Toward the end of their kingdoms, when they have become morally rotten, an angry king shall rise to power with great shrewdness and intelligence. His power shall be mighty, but it will be satanic strength and not his own.

Prospering wherever he turns, he will destroy all who oppose him, though their armies be mighty, and he will devastate God's people." The Antichrist's arrival shall be earth shaking to say the least. He shall aide in the peaceful settlement of international disputes with his advice on restoring law and order, inspiring many with sensible and reasonable changes of peace and equality. Gaining the trust and respect of many and with a growing number of followers the world over, a few people particularly those of the western alliance shall realize he is not what he appears to be and his intensions are not quite so honorable. As the new center of attention his "meddling in human affairs" may behind closed doors create grudging admiration leading to the long hidden friction of mistrust between Beauty and the Beast. For it is America the beautiful who sits upon her worldly throne with delight guiding and watching over her vast modern civilization. Both sides shall observe each other with great interest. However, on the outside America at that point in history shall be tied down by world pressure of opinion with the very UN/NWO laws she helped to create and establish. America shall be placed in a position of weakness and no longer from a position of strength. The Beast shall have the upper hand on all fronts as he gradually alienates and isolates the western powers from the rest of the world. America shall be viewed as a cruel oppressor, bully, and deceitful warmonger. The resentment of many shall linger over her. The Beast on the other hand shall be viewed as a savior of humanity and wise leader. Viewed as shrewd and highly intelligent his impressionable power few shall realize is satanic. The spiritually awaken shall gain understanding and realize the earth is not big enough

for the two. The Beast has America in his crosshairs and war is imminent. The final showdown has begun.

In the beginning of world peace and rebuilding with very few taken notice the Beast (who has realized his difficulties with the United States and her allies) shall confer with powerful adversaries of the west. In the descriptions of Daniel 9:27: "he will put an end to sacrifice and offerings." A gradual change in the beginning many will not know what to make of him. The Beast shall gain the trust of many and people who in turn will abandon their old fashion religions to worship their new discovered hope and his unaccustomed covenant. By making such bold moves upon a world rich in many ancient religions and traditions which solely rely upon sacrifice and offerings may only be seen as the start of a global over throw.

Acts 17:24 (New International Version) – "The God who made the world and everything in it is the Lord of heaven and earth and does not live in temples built by human hands." There is a misconception about the temple described in Daniel 9:27. The temple referred is not a manmade structure built and erected with human hands from materials of the earth. Rather the human heart created by God which is the temple described suitable for his Holy Spirit to dwell. And the Beast Antichrist shall in a clever manner create a perfect mixture of lies and truth to confuse and deceive a weary people so he may advance slowly, working his way into the temple of each human heart with vain ideas of flattery and false promises. Only to create, arrange and camouflage an abomination of evil that shall influence and convince many people to leave their beliefs and stop the daily sacrifices and offerings to

the true God of heaven. The following consequences shall cause an abomination and gradual isolation of desolation creating a spiritual emptiness ridding the temple of all purity. The definition of desolate: *act of desolating; a desolate state or place; afflicted; forlorn; melancholy.* The definition of forlorn: *deserted; abandoned; miserable.* To add insult to injury following the third world war overthrow of the whole earth the Antichrist's true colors of influence and deceit first taken notice by the spiritually awaken shall create an intensifying struggle between the two. Forcing upon the nations his laws and requirements for all to obey without question. The appearance and works of the Antichrist before and after this devastating war proves once and for all many already serving within the established worldwide Apostate Church originally created by the Mighty Babylon shall be lured farther away from the Lord with the Beast's hollow promises of vanity. Into the miserable, melancholy prison of desolation to become even more profoundly indifferent to the eternal will of God within the heart, mind and soul. And many shall blindly stubborn themselves in the Antichrist's deceit as the Beast convinces the nations to soldier on even in the face of many natural and spiritual calamities.

Daniel 8:25 (King James Version) - "And through his policy also he shall magnify himself in his heart, and by peace shall destroy many; he shall also stand up against the Prince of princes; but he shall be broken without hand." A master of deception the Beast shall destroy many spiritually knowing very well he has tricked and enticed many around the globe with his policy or covenant and fraudulent speech. The Beast shall (before and after the war) extol himself

as he witnesses to his amazement the crafty skill of management to his strategic plans against mankind materializing beyond expectations. The deceit of the Beast-Antichrist (Mighty Demon of War) shall destroy many others spiritually and with the Mighty Demons of famine, death and hell of the third world war to follow. Antichrist shall magnify himself to an extent he (through his careless mockery towards the heavenly host) shall even challenge the Prince of princes, the Lord and Savior Jesus Christ the son of the eternal God himself.

In the beginning the plans of the UN/NWO shall appear to be succeeding. With few understanding the United States has become trapped and bound in a vulnerable worldwide strategic disadvantage at every level. The faithful shall awaken and recognize the dangers only to realize they have one final opportunity to heed the warnings. With certain brave individuals quoting prophetic verses. And they shall relay many messages to all peoples high and low. Some losing their mortal lives in the process. Then without warning the Antichrist will destroy many by peace with the terrible sudden destruction of world war III. And to maintain his glory in the eyes of many shall mix lies with truth bringing forth before the world his profound compounded evidence and reasons for doing so. Diverting the course of the NWO and luring the people of the earth down the road to the age and worship of the Antichrist and the Great Tribulations of horror to follow.

To give a brief summary of the Ram and the Goat shall be interchangeable fellowship offering sacrifice to create a more harmonies New World Order among all nations lead and supervised by the United Nations

assembly (the inspiration and creation of the western powers). The sudden long expected change shall result in widespread fighting and bloodshed attracting a false peacemaker - the Antichrist. The Beast shall aid in the mending and healing between the nations winning many people over with his lies all the while plotting man's destruction isolating the west creating a growing mistrust of the western powers eventually leading to the third world war overthrow.

History teaches manmade power and glory is fleeting. The illusion of a romantic never ending story of one world trading partners mingling in their economic, political and strategic marriage as the world move toward a bright future of global security is nothing more than a fool's paradise. The truth Antichrist, the Prince of the bottomless pit is a fraudulent master strategist skilled in the arts of war, leadership and deception who at the opportune moment shall arrive as a wolf in sheep's clothing. Enticing his peaceful solutions upon a weary people and setting the New World Order of universal peace and harmony in motion all the while plotting mankind's destruction. His name Revelation 9:11 in Hebrew is Abaddon and in Greek is Apollyon. Translated "the destroyer," God's battle ax and sword upon a rebellious world.

Daniel 12:4 (Modern Translation) - "But Daniel, keep this prophecy a secret; seal it up so that it will not be understood until the end times, when travel and education shall be vastly increased!"

America's Last Stand

Before moving to the Mighty Demons, there is the matter of the first rider. Questions remain in the minds of some who the particular rider may be. The highlights underlined of the following scriptures make it abundantly clear. The mysterious rider sitting upon a white horse (white is the sign of purity) with the armies of heaven following him and crowned with many victories to win the war against sin is the Lord Jesus himself.

Revelation 6:2 (Modern Translation) - "I looked, and there in front of me was a white horse. Its rider carried a bow, and a crown was placed upon his head; he rode out to conquer in many battles and win the war."

Revelation 19:11 (Modern Translation) - "Then I saw heaven opened and a white horse standing there; and the one sitting on the horse was named Faithful and True the one who justly punishes and makes war."

Revelation 19:13 (Modern Translation) - "He was clothed with garments dipped in blood, and his title was The Word of God."

Revelation 19:14 (Modern Translation) - "The armies of heaven, dressed in finest linen, white and clean, followed him on white horses."

Revelation 19:16 (Modern Translation) - "On his robe and thigh was written this title: "King of Kings and Lord of Lords."

THE MIGHTY DEMONS

Revelation 6:4 (Modern Translation) - "This time a red horse rode out. Its rider was given a long sword and the authority to banish peace and bring anarchy to the earth; war and killing broke out everywhere." The Mighty Demon is without a doubt the Antichrist following closely behind him: Famine, Death, and Hell.

Revelation 6:5 (Modern Translation) - "When he had broken the third seal, I heard the third Living Being say, "Come!" And I saw a black horse, with its rider holding a pair a balances in his hand." Famine.

Revelation 6:8 (Modern Translation) - "And I looked, and behold a pale horse; and his name that sat on him was Death and Hell followed with him. And power was given unto them over the fourth part of the earth, to kill with sword, and with hunger, and with death, and with the beasts of the earth."

The Mighty Demons are given control over the "Fourth" part of the earth or the last to be internationally established - North and South America. The Mighty Demons have the power to kill with sword (war), with hunger (famine), with death (followed by hell), and with beasts. The definition of beast: *any four footed animal; a brutal man*. Following the third world war, the intense famine may force many to become beasts of prey. Man and animal alike.

Canada geographically positioned due north of the United States may suffer the same fate. North America is bordered in a triangular formation extending from Greenland to Alaska and narrowing down to Panama. The two national bodies of this continent the United States and Canada are under extreme scrutiny and targeted more than any other location on earth.

England (estranged from their European neighbors) is politically knitted in as an existing member of the European Union. Nevertheless England stands steadfastly united with the Western alliance. Jeremiah 50:12 (King James Version) - "Your mother shall be sore confounded; she that bare you shall be ashamed; behold, the hindermost of the nations shall be a wilderness, a dry land, and a desert." England the Mother Lion shall be sorely or severely distressed in their grief. Confounded or in other words astounded and confused in their overthrow. With no American military support and or economic aid to arrive. England in their despair gaze to the west over the annihilation of their closest allies with the reign of the Antichrist secure, the remainder of the earth now realizes the fate of any who resist.

The fortunate few chosen to survive within the ruins of the once mighty lands of North America shall be taken away as slaves. For God has chosen some to survive, Only God knows who. The large number of souls caught off guard at the war's beginning who lose their mortal lives shall be feed to the horseman Death and finally Hell.

Revelation 18:8 (Modern Translation) - "Therefore the sorrows of death and mourning and famine shall overtake her in a single day, and she shall be

utterly consumed by fire; for mighty is the Lord who judges her."

Revelation 9:14 (Modern Translation) - "saying to the sixth angel, "Release the four mighty demons held bound at the great river Euphrates." They had been kept in readiness for that year and month and day and hour, and now they were turned loose to kill a third of all mankind. They lead an army of 200,000,000 warriors - I heard an announcement of how many there were."

The Mighty Demons ride leading the ten nation armies known as the Locusts. A vast military machine racing across the land, sea and air as the nations of the earth quake in terror at the site of their presence as they rush into battle.

The Flaming Arrows

Jeremiah 50:9 (Modern Translation) - "For see, I am raising up an army of great nations from the north and I will bring them against Babylon to attack her and she shall be destroyed. The enemy's arrows go straight to the mark; they don't miss!" The arrows represent nuclear missiles known for their accuracy (most having a multiple warhead design). Russia and China considered two obvious choices of the great northern nations, both economic and military world powers. At the precise time shall be ordered to unleash their nuclear arsenal with a brilliantly planned and co-ordinated overwhelming surprise nuclear attack. Carpet bombing the entire landscape with a huge barrage of nuclear might, leaving everything

destroyed. The moment all skillfully offensive strategic chess moves have been accomplished to create such a successful attack the Mighty Demons shall be unleashed leading a mighty conventional force.

Matthew 24:29 (Modern Translation) - "Immediately after the persecution of those days the sun will be darkened, and the moon will not give light and the stars will seem to fall from the heavens, and the powers overshadowing the earth will convulsed." The image of stars falling from the heavens is the symbolic representation of nuclear war. With both nations, America and Russia positioned on complete opposite sides of the globe. The obvious time to strike the west would be at America's slowest reaction time in the early morning hours. The sun becoming darkened and the moon that will not give light may refer (with many wild fires burning out of control over such a large portion of land) to the tons of nuclear fallout thrown into the atmosphere creating a deadly nuclear winter after effect. Mixing in with the west to east atmospheric winds circulating the globe for a prolong period of time shall cause the sun and moon to appear blacked out and at times blood red. The powers overshadowing the earth will convulse. Luke 21:26 (Modern Translation) - "the stability of the heavens will be broken up." Isaiah gave a more vivid description: Isaiah 13:13 (Modern Translation) - "For I will shake the heavens in my wrath and fierce anger, and the earth will move from its place in the skies." The demonstrations of their nuclear deterrent shall have a terrible impact on the earth's fragile environment it shall disrupt the balance of nature. The global sphere upon which we live shall gradually move from its orbit and or tilted off its axis, something to this effect. Following these terrible

events at God's chosen time shall the natural plagues or judgments described by Nostradamus, Edgar Casey and the Prophets of the Holy Bible among others fulfilled. And as time progresses these natural disasters shall be worldwide and shall intensify growing more frequently destructive.

Century II, Quatrain 91:
At the rising of the sun a great fire,
shall be seen, noise and light tending to the North,
within the round, death and cries shall be heard,
death by sword, fire, hunger watching for them.

Century V, Quatrain 8:
The fire shall be left burning, the dead shall be hid,
within the globes terrible and fearful,
by night the fleet shall shoot against the city,
the city shall be on fire, the enemy shall be favorable to it.

By night the fleet shall shoot their ballistic missiles at The Great New City. And at the rising of the sun or early morning nuclear attacks accompanied by ear piercing noise and blinding light shall be seen. Within the round or globes of the mushroom cloud death and cries terrible, fearful shall be heard. The dead hidden beneath the burning rubble as the land undefended is wide open to enemy invasion. Each quatrain represents numerous early morning strikes. A military attack may begin with a huge naval force. The most feared of the sea would be the submarine. The SLBM or Submarine Launched Ballistic Missile attacks.

Revelation 8:8-9 (King James Version) - "And the second angel sounded, and as it were, a great mountain burning with fire was cast into the sea, and the third

part of the sea became blood. And the third part of the creatures which were in the sea, and had life; died and the third part of the ships were destroyed." The great burning mountain or continent is North America following the barrage of nuclear strikes. The Great Shinning New City sitting upon the Great Mountain is cast down from their heights of authority, glory and power into the sea-the sea of nations. The third part of the creatures that had died is the third part of mankind dead in the sea of nations. The third part of the sea becoming blood is another description of one-third of mankind dying in this horrible war. Along with the nuclear armament the engagements of fierce naval battles shall destroy a third part of the ships. Commercial shipping, ships privately owned and or ships of leisure. America has the most active ports in the world. Jeremiah 51:13 (Modern Translation) - "O Wealthy port, great center of commerce your end has come; the thread of your life is cut."

Isaiah 13:7 (Modern Translation) - "Your arms lie paralyzed with fear; the strongest hearts melt, and are afraid. Fear grips you with terrible pangs, like those of a woman in labor. You look at one another helpless, as the flames of the burning city reflect upon your pallid faces." After the nuclear attacks have ceased, with the fire storm raging out of control the fortunate few alive shall arise from their shelters of safety and wander in shock and dismay.

Century I, Quatrain 91:
The gods shall make it appear to mankind,
that they are the authors of a great war,
the sky that was serene shall show sword, and lance,
on the left hand the affliction shall be greater.

The gods or the ten kings will make it appear that they are the planners of a great-war, World War III. In reality the master planner of a full scale war is the Antichrist. The sky once serene is now filled with countless missiles and warplanes. The left hand affliction may be a geographical reference. If you review a modern world map, the west is usually on the left side.

A REPEAT OF HISTORY

Isaiah 13:19 (Modern Translation) - "And so Babylon, the most glorious of kingdoms, the flower of Chaldean culture will be as utterly destroyed as Sodom and Gomorrah were when God sent fire from heaven."

Jeremiah 50:40 (Modern Translation) - "The Lord declares that he will destroy Babylon just as he destroyed Sodom and Gomorrah and their neighboring towns. No one has lived in them since, and no one will live again in Babylon."

The terrible fire storm devouring everything and everyone before it leaving in its wake famine, suffering and death leaves the job half done. The second of the two horrors quickly follows. A full scale armed invasion of conventional forces lead by the Mighty Demons. To insure the land is cleaned out of all her wealth and power.

Ten nations strong or as these armies are known: The Locusts. Revelation chapter eight describes the nuclear strikes. Revelation chapter nine describes the invasion of conventional armed forces to follow.

THE LOCUSTS

Revelation 9:7-10 (Modern Translation) - "The locusts looked like horses armored for battle. They had what looked like golden crowns on their heads, and their faces looked like men's. Their hair was long like women, and their teeth were those of lions. They wore breastplates that seemed to be of iron, and their wings roared like an army of chariots rushing into battle. They had stinging tails like scorpions, and their power to hurt, given to them for five months, was in their tails." The Locusts appear as armored horses or tanks and other military armored vehicles. The gold crown upon the heads of the Locusts is symbolic. The definition of crown: *an ornament for the head in the form of a wreath; a badge of royalty; perfection; completion; to finish; to perfection.* Antichrist's well-oiled war machine is at its full completion. Trained and polished to military perfection, a crowning achievement for many generations of hard brutal work upon the Fourth Wild Beast. Rise above any and all challenges the Locusts crowned or surmounted with many overcoming combat victories for their sacrifices. Their faces appear as men, men of many races and nationality who operate all military equipment. Their hair was long as women. Hair is a symbol of beauty. In contrast, it is also the object of rebellion when the youth of the 1960's rebelled against authority, law and order. They let their hair grow. I Corinthians 11:14-15 (Modern Translation) - "Does not even instinct itself teach us that women's heads should be covered? For women are proud of their long hair, while a man with long hair tends to be ashamed." As the youth in the 1960's the Locusts rebel against God and the laws he has set in place. Their teeth reveal to the advancing

highly trained military armed forces devouring everything before them. Towns and cities attacked with war, pillaging and looting shall fall before them. The Locusts have wings signifies aircraft. The breastplates are their protection (which I will explain in detail the next paragraph). The Locusts have the power to hurt men for five months. During the time of Noah, God destroyed mankind with a flood. God is allowing the Locusts to hurt mankind by destroying one third of the world's population. And this particular war will last five months hurting mankind with the stings of many battles.

Revelation 9:17-19 (Modern Translation) - "I saw their horses spread out before me in my vision; their riders wore fiery-red breastplates, though some were sky blue and others yellow. The horse heads looked much like lions and smoke and fire and flaming sulphur billowed from their mouths, killing one-third of all mankind. Their power of death was not only in their mouths, but in their tails as well, for their tails were similar to serpent heads that struck and bit with fatal wounds." The breastplates in ancient times were used to protect the warrior. The Locusts breastplates are fiery-red, sky-blue and yellow, the breastplates in relation with the fire (red breastplate) and flaming sulphur billowing from their mouths. The different colors refer to the basic elements of gunpowder. The definition of gunpowder: *an explosive mixture of saltpeter, sulphur and charcoal.* The definition of sulphur: *brimstone; a simple mineral substance of a yellow color* (yellow breastplate) *which burns with a pale-blue* (sky-blue breastplate) *flame.* The Locust's protective breastplates or offensive and defensive weapons of war create the power of death also in their tails. The Locusts leave behind a trail of

total destruction, with the fatal wounds of mourning, suffering and death.

Isaiah 41:5-7 (Modern Translation) - "The lands beyond the sea watch in fear and wait for word of Cyrus's new campaigns. Remote lands tremble and mobilize for war. The craftsmen encourage each other as they rush to make new idols to protect them. The carver hurries the goldsmith and the molder helps at the anvil. "Good," they say. "It's coming along fine. Now we can solder on the arms." Carefully they join the parts together, and then fasten the thing in place so it won't fall over!" The lands of North America beyond the seas of the ancient world the people wander and watch helplessly in their burning land. They wait in terror for new planned attacks. America trembles and gathers what forces she can for war to defend herself. They try to open up their demolished factories and put into production their idols to protect themselves. Their tanks and war planes, and weapons of all kinds emptying out any and all warehouses of useful military arms in mothball retirement supplies and or ammunition dumps. Time has now run-out. The Locusts are on the move.

Joel 2:3-5 (Modern Translation) - "Fire goes before them and follows them on every side. Ahead of them the land lies fair as Eden's Garden in all its beauty, but they destroy it to the ground; not one thing escapes. They look like tiny horses, and they run as fast. Look at them leaping along the tops of the mountains! Listen to the noise they make like the rumbling of chariots, or the roar of fire sweeping across a field, and like a mighty army moving into battle." Nuclear fire devours before the Locusts and follows them on every side. The

land ahead of them, which is as fair as Eden's Garden, is North America. And yet it is destroyed to the ground, and not one thing escapes. These armored Locusts spread out are armored vehicles of all types and they move with tremendous speed. The Locusts also have wings and are leaping along the tops of the mountains is once again referring to aircraft. With a thundering noise the huge military war machine of Locusts swarm over the land as a dark cloud.

Isaiah 13:14-15 (Modern Translation) - "The armies of Babylon will run until exhausted, fleeing back to their own land like deer chased by dogs, wandering like sheep deserted by their shepherd. Those who don't run will be butchered." The American armed forces retreat is a full scale route pushed back to their homeland from every direction by the Locusts strong advancement. Many American and allied troops desert and wander in dismay and confusion. And those stopping to rest or surrender are massacred.

Jeremiah 51:30,32 (Modern Translation) - "Her mightiest soldiers no longer fight they stay in their barracks. Their courage is gone; they have become as women. The invaders have burned the houses and broken down the city gates. Messengers from every side come running to the king to tell him all is lost! All the escape routes are blocked; the fortifications are burning and the army is in panic." As the Locusts are advancing closer and closer to the American homeland hope fades. The courage of many fails them aids from all over report the war is lost. There is no support or chance of escape.

Isaiah 13:16 (Modern Translation) - "Their little children will be dashed to death against the pavement right before their eyes; their homes will be sacked, and their wives raped by the attacking hordes." The Locusts storm the beaches of several coastlines. In their fury commit unspeakable crimes to the population the young and old, rich and poor, authority and private citizen alike. The fighting of opposing armies in the cities and towns as around the world is ferocious. From street to street and house to house, the advancing Locusts pushing their way farther and deeper into North American territory from all sides to link up their forces.

Jeremiah 50:30,37 (Modern Translation) - "Her young men will fall in the streets and die, her warriors will all be killed. War shall devour her horses and chariots, and her allies from other lands shall become as weak as women. Her treasures shall all be robbed." Once the Locusts have gained a foothold they fight and push further inland, looting and pillaging (hidden and well known) North American treasuries homes and businesses of the rich and poor alike. Anything and everything of value shall be taken.

Century X, Quatrain 81:
A treasure put in a temple by Hesperian citizens,
in the same hid in a secret place,
the hungry serfs shall cause the temple to be open,
and take again and ravish, a fearful prey in the middle.

The definition of Hesperian: *western; situated at the west.* A treasure put in a temple or bank(s) by the Hesperian or Western citizens is hidden in the secret place or vaults. The hungry Serfs or Villains or

Locusts shall break in and steal all the riches. Caught in the middle of all this horror are countless frighten Hesperian peoples, prey for the onslaught of Locusts. Nostradamus foresaw the looting and pillaging of banks and other bigger and lesser prizes. I Corinthians 3:16 (King James Version) - "Know ye not that ye are the temple of God, and that the Spirit of God dwells in you?" The human heart is the temple of your beliefs. In other words "Home is where the heart is." The largest of these desired treasures of coarse are those of the Hesperian's sacred beliefs that dwell in the secret place or temple of their heart of hearts.

Jeremiah 50:10 (Modern Translation) - "And Babylon shall be sacked until everyone is sated with loot, says the Lord." The third world war with the Hesperian's has ended and their enemies roars of victory lift up to the heavens. The scorched lands shall be littered with bodies, from the intense fighting. Victory celebrations shall be held, and the Locusts take their loot, trophies and slaves, women and children alike with them. The North American highway systems cleared of all debris and bodies shall be filled with military convoys flowing back and forth to awaiting cargo ships and planes until the modern woman is stripped of all wealth. Nothing of value remains.

Jeremiah 50:39 (Modern Translation) - "Therefore this city of Babylon shall become inhabited by ostriches and jackals; it shall be a home for the wild animals of the desert. Never again shall it be lived in by human beings; it shall lie desolate forever." The land of milk and honey, and now the land of nothing a desolate everlasting waste identical to the land of Sodom and Gomorrah. Once the beautiful palaces and mansions

are now inhabited by the birds and wild animals. At night not a single man made light is seen anywhere. The howling creatures of the darkness cry out. The dust covered wind thrown upon the ruins. Thorns and nettles over run the once magnificent state and federal buildings.

Jeremiah 51:26 (Modern Translation) - "You shall be desolate forever; even your stones shall never be used for building again. You shall be completely wiped out. Abandon forever!" The Great New City is reduced to a ghost town. Her judgments never end. In those future days, ships and their captains and crew sail by her shores at a safe distance and whistle and mock her desolate ruins. Watching the smoke ascent toward the heavens they shake their heads in disbelief over all her destruction. America's sins shall be a reminder to the world never stray from the path of God.

Century III, Quatrain 84:
The great city shall be made very desolate,
not one of the inhabitants shall be left in it,
wall, sex, church and virgin ravished,
by sword, fire, plague, cannon, people shall die.

The prophets of the Holy Bible and Nostradamus have written down similar prophetic visions. Proof their knowledge was received from the same source, the Lord. The Great New City shall be made very desolate by fire, sword, plague, canon from the horrid nightmare of the third world war.

The Two Witnesses

Revelation 11:3 (Modern Translation) - "And I will give power unto my two witnesses, and they shall prophesy a thousand two hundred and threescore days, clothed in sackcloth."

Revelation 11:7 (King James Version) - "And when they shall have finished their testimony, the beast that ascendeth out of the bottomless pit shall make war against them, and shall overcome them, and kill them."

Revelation 11:8 (King James Version) - "And their dead bodies shall lie in the street of the "Great City" which spiritually is called Sodom and Egypt, where also our Lord was crucified."

Revelation 11:11 (King James Version) - "And after three days and a half the spirit of life from God entered into them, and they stood upon their feet; and great fear fell upon them which saw them."

Revelation 11:12 (King James Version) - "And they heard a great voice from heaven saying unto them, "Come up hither." And they ascended up to heaven in a cloud; and their enemies beheld them."

The two witnesses decent from heaven approximately the same time the Antichrist is ascending from the abyss to organize and prepare any details for the final creation of his ten nation alliance. They shall prophesy one thousand two hundred and threescore or sixty days and during their testimony they shall command any plague they wish. The two witnesses shall reveal all God's well hidden prophetical plans

for the very near future. At the end of their testimony, Antichrist attacks the two witnesses as they dwell in the Great New City and kills them at the start of the third world war. Their dead bodies lie in the street of the Great New City of the West. Corrupt to the core by her vast supreme power. John 14:6 (King James Version) - "Jesus said unto him, I am the way, the truth, and the life; no man cometh unto the Father, but by me." She crucified the Lord of truth (in other words murdered the truth with her veil of silence is golden rule in order to live a profitable luxurious existence in denial of God) in her very streets or lands and system of laws and daily life creating herself into the many images of Sodom and Egypt.

Three and one half days (following the nuclear cease fire) the Hesperian or Norman peoples await Antichrist's new planned attacks. In the midst of the ruins filled with thick black smoke and the stench of death what was once The Great New City. The Lord breath's life back into the two witnesses and they stand up. And all those who witness this miracle shall be overshadowed with fear and awe. Their eyes shall be opened, learning to late of God. Then the Lord calls upon the two witnesses, "Come up here!" As the two prophets begin ascending to heaven, the people gather to stare in disbelief and cry out to them. For they know their fate is sealed. Antichrist and his vast military machine are on the way. Do not let this happen to you!

A MESSAGE TO THE ELITE

Isaiah 28:15 (New International Version) - "You boast, "We have entered into a covenant with death, with the realm of the dead we have made an agreement. When

an overwhelming scourge sweeps by, it cannot touch us, for we have made a lie our refuge and falsehood our hiding place."

Isaiah 5:8-9 (Modern Translation) - "You buy up property so others have no place to live. Your homes are built on great estates so you can be alone in the midst of the earth! But the Lord Almighty has sworn your awful fate - with my own ears I heard him say, "Many a beautiful home will lie deserted, their owners killed or gone."

Isaiah 47:1-3 (Modern Translation) - "O Babylon, the unconquered, come sit in the dust; for your days of glory, pomp and honor are ended. O daughter of Chaldea, never again will you be the lovely princess, tender and delicate. Take heavy millstones and grind the corn; remove your veil; strip off your robe; expose yourself to public view. You shall be in nakedness and shame. I will take vengeance upon you and will not repent."

Daniel 2:27-28 (Modern Translation) - "Daniel replied, "No wise man, astrologer, magician, or wizard can tell the king such things, but there is a God in heaven who reveals secrets, and he has told you in your dream what will happen in the future."

Matthew 10:26 (Modern Translation) - "But don't be afraid of those who threaten you. For the time is coming when the truth will be revealed: their secret plots will become public information."

Revelation 18:9-11 (Modern Translation) - "And the world leaders, who took part in her immoral acts

and enjoyed her favors, will mourn for her as they see the smoke rising from her charred remains. They will stand far off, trembling with fear and crying out, "Alas, Babylon, that mighty city! In one moment her judgment fell. The merchants of the earth will weep and mourn for her, for there is no one left to buy their goods."

Revelation 18:15-17 (Modern Translation) - "And so the merchants who have become wealthy by selling her these things shall stand at a distance, fearing danger to themselves, weeping and crying, Alas, that great city, so beautiful - like a woman clothed in finest purple and scarlet linens, decked out with gold and precious stones and pearls! In one moment, all the wealth of the city is gone!"

Revelation 6:15-17 (Modern Translation) - "The Kings of the earth, and world leaders and rich men and high ranking military officers, and all men great and small, slave and free, hid themselves in the caves and rocks of the mountains, and cried to the mountains to crush them. "Fall on us," they pleaded, and hide us from the face of the one sitting on the throne, and from the anger of the Lamb, because the great day of their anger has come, and who can survive it?"

Isaiah 2:19-22 (Modern Translation) - "When the Lord stands up from his throne to shake up the earth, his enemies will crawl with fear into the holes in the rocks and into the caves because of the glory of his majesty. Then at last they will abandon their gold and silver idols to the moles and bats, and crawl into the caverns to hide among the jagged rocks at the tops of the cliffs to try to get away from the terror of the Lord and the

glory of his majesty when he rises to terrify the earth. Puny man! Frail as his breath! Don't ever put your trust in him!"

Revelation 20:11-12 (Modern Translation) - "And I saw a great white throne and the one who sat upon it, from whose face the earth and sky fled away, but they found no place to hide. I saw the dead, great and small, standing before God; and The Books were opened, including the Book of Life. And the dead were judged according to the things written in The Books, each according to the deeds he had done."

My words within this section shall be few. Nevertheless the Lord's warnings remain abundantly clear.

The Aftermath

Revelation 13:14 (Modern Translation) - "He did unbelievable miracles such as making fire flame down to earth from the skies while everyone was watching. By doing these miracles, he was deceiving people everywhere. He could do these marvelous things whenever the first creature was there to watch him. And he ordered the people of the world to make a great statue of the first creature who was fatally wounded and then came back to life." The scripture is revealing the Antichrist and his ten nation alliance possess the high tech and nuclear capability. In the aftermath of world war III mankind now faces the dread of more retaliation. The Beast shall exercise his ability to flex their military muscle in a necessary show of brute force against any opposing foe skillfully scared in the minds of a conquered unsuspecting world now under the domain of the Antichrist. Fear mingled with intimating displays of incredible power is a persuasive form of mind control. The Antichrist has endless diabolical tools necessary to create a lasting image or statue to his own likeness. With the Beast's powerful earthly foes quickly destroyed and removed from the world stage including the success of each won event quickly overlap another. Antichrist becomes more over confident with pride and arrogance. This angry king (following the defeat of the two witnesses) attempts to create (through a lasting impression of superior knowledge and power) the blinding illusion he is Lord and Savior of the planet. Matthew 24:15-16 – (Modern Translation) – "So, when you see the horrible thing (told about by Daniel the prophet) standing in the holy place (Note to the reader: you know what is meant!) those in Judea must flee into the Judean hills." In the beginning Antichrist shall create what man has failed to accomplish in the holy land. Peace between the big three religions consisting of the Jews, Christians and the Muslims. Many around the world shall gratefully open the temple of their hearts to him and in their overwhelming joy shall erect manmade temples globally in his honor for the Christ like return and intervention for world peace. It has been said time and again that one percent of the world population owns over ninety five percent of the world's wealth. The ancient tactic of the Beast-Antichrist is he shall lead the poor of the world to victory against "The Great New City," "The Mighty Invincible Babylon" – "The United States, the land of wealth and pride" and she shall suffer a humiliating revolutionary defeat at the hands of the poor. In the aftermath of world war III his careless reassurance in evil's false security continues to grow and strengthen as the poor and forgotten who have had their sweet tastes of political and military victories against the Western powers shall at the peak of their overflowing joy worship the Beast-Antichrist as their Lord and Savior for his brilliant leadership and flawless military planning. The Antichrist in the beginning shall be viewed as a liberator from the "Great Suppresser" America. And to ensnare the world's population even more into his web of deceit, the Beast shall spread the wealth to anyone who is willing to follow and worship him. To gain even more reinforcing support the Antichrist shall reveal the hidden national secrets of the western alliance. At the peak of all his terrible deeds the Antichrist physically enters and defiles the holy land of Israel as

his own and into the holy city of Jerusalem ending all spiritual and traditional exhibited religious sacrifices, a desolating sacrilege spreading across the entire world. Challenging and mocking the very authority of heaven setting the stage for the final showdown with the true Lord of all creation. And to those living in the Holy land of Israel the arrival of the Beast-Antichrist and the revealing of his evil nature and conduct is a warning sign to flee to the Judean hills for safety.

Revelation 13:3-4 (Modern Translation) - "I saw that one of his heads seemed wounded beyond recovery-but the fatal wound was healed! All the world marveled at this miracle and followed the creature in awe. They worshiped the Dragon for giving him such power, and they worshiped the Strange Creature. "Where is there anyone as great as he?" They exclaimed. Who is able to fight against him?" The wounded head recovered is a description of the Antichrist's resurrection from the dead. The world marveled at this miracle and followed the creature (Antichrist) in awe. The definition of marvel: *a wonder; something very astonishing; to feel admiration or astonishment.* The definition of astonish: *to surprise; amazement.* The definition of admiration: *wonder mingled with delight; esteem.* The definition of admire: *to regard with delight or affection.* The definition of admirer: *one who admires; a lover.* The definition of esteem: *to set a value on; to regard with respect; to prize.* The remaining global sea of nations their hearts filled with bereavement search in desperation (fear the Antichrist preys upon) for leadership to guide them from troubling uncertain times. Standing before them, people from all walks of life shall witness and listen to the victorious Beast Antichrist in all his false hopes of glory. And through his clever, persuasive deceit of

brainwashing oration desperate multitudes (who so easily deceived with corruption) begin changing their minds. Sinking further into a vulnerable trap the sea of nations awe inspired admire and follow the Strange Creature - Antichrist in a esteem and astonishing way it leads to worshipping him. And without realizing it through their thoughts and course of action they love and worship the Dragon (Satan). Where is it lead to? Receive the mark of the Beast.

Revelation 13:16 (King James Version) - "and he cause all, both small and great, rich and poor, free and bond to receive a mark in their right hand or in their foreheads." Not on but in their foreheads. In other words, in the memory of their collective subconscious thinking they profoundly love and worship the beast. That in a nutshell is taking the mark of the Beast, a continuing battle for control of the mind.

Take the mark of the Beast in the right hand. The definition of in: ***within; inside of; in or within some place, state, circumstances.*** **The definition of inside:** ***in the interior of; within.*** **The definition of within:** ***in the interior of; in the compass of.*** **The definition of compass:** ***an instrument for directing the course; to contrive.*** **The definition of contrive:** ***to invent; to devise; to form or design.*** **The definition of devise:** ***to form in the mind; to invent.*** **The definition of invent:** ***to devise or produce as something new; to fabricate.*** **The definition of fabricate:** ***to make or fashion; to form by art or labor; to devise falsely.***

The definition of right: ***belonging to that side of the body farther from the heart; authority.*** **The definition of authority:** ***influence conferred by character.*** **The**

definition of confer: ***to consult together; to give or bestow; to apply.*** **The definition of apply:** ***to use; to employ; to solicit.*** **The definition of solicit:** ***to invite.***

The definition of right-hand: ***essentially needful or serviceable.*** **The definition of serviceable:** ***that renders service; useful; beneficial.*** **The definition of useful:** ***valuable for use; advantageous.*** **The definition of benefit:** ***an act of kindness; a favor; to do a service to; to gain advantage.*** **The definition of advantage:** ***favorable state; superiority; gain; to promote.*** **The definition of promote:** ***to forward or further; to advance; to encourage; to exalt; to form a company.*** **The definition of exalt:** ***to raise high; to raise to power or dignity; to extol.*** **The definition of extol:** ***to magnify; to glorify.***

The definition of hand: ***the extremity of the arm, consisting of the palm and fingers; skill; power; belonging to.*** **The definition of belong:** ***to be the property; to appertain; to be connected.*** **The definition of appertain:** ***to belong; to relate.*** **The definition of relate:** ***to tell; to narrate; to ally by kindred; to refer; to stand in some relation.*** **The definition of ally:** ***to unite by friendship; marriage or treaty; to associate.*** **The definition of associate:** ***to join in company with; a companion; friend.*** **The definition of unite:** ***to combine; to connect; to associate; to become one.*** **The definition of connect:** ***to conjoin; to combine; to associate; to unite or cohere together; to have a close relation.*** **The definition of cohere:** ***to stick together; to be consistent.*** **The definition of consistent:** ***fixed; firm; not contradictory.*** **The definition of conjoin:** ***to join together; to unite; to associate.*** **The definition of combine:** ***to cause to unite; to join; to come into union; to coalesce; to league together; a union.*** **The definition of coalesce:** ***to grow together; to unite.***

Hand definitions continued: The definition of skill: *ability; knowledge united with dexterity; aptitude*. The definition of aptitude: *fitness; readiness*. The definition of dexterity: *right-handedness; adroitness; expertness*. The definition of power: *ability to act or do; strengthen; influence; talent; command; authority; one who exercise authority; a state or government; a mechanical advantage; product of the multiplication of a number by itself*. The definition of influence: *agency or power serving to affect; modify; sway; effect; acknowledged ascendency with people in power; to exercise influence on; to bias; to sway*. The definition of influential: *exerting influence physical or other; possessing power*. The definition of sway: *to swing or vibrate; to incline; to govern; to wield; to influence; to rule; preponderance; ascendency*. The definition of preponderant: *superior in power; influence; to exceed in influence or power*. The definition of ascendency: *controlling power; sway; rising; superiority*.

History reveals conclusively all official decisions of national interest declared by the leading powers governing to be passed down and circulated among the general population. The Antichrist's global strategic plans bear no exception to the rule.

The latest set of definitions reveals a solid foundation of obedience to the Antichrist. The Antichrist's new laws of influence shall be passed down through the False Prophet to the right-hand authority figures seated into their positions of power of each and every national Government, Province, State, city, town, village, tribal, family, around the world.

All existing positions exhibiting powers of authority around the globe is solely reserved for only the most loyal to the Beast. Anyone disrupting the

Antichrist's changes at any time shall be removed and prisoned with possible life threatening termination (Revelation 13:15) as a strict example and stern warning to all forms of treason once the vacant seats of power have become occupied. The right-hand authority figures shall receive the Beast's commands declaring his changes of all morals and laws. In turn the right-hand authority figures shall sow the very seeds in the minds of the global populations.

The selected right-hand authority figures chosen for a special service to the Beast are then marked with Antichrist's personal endorsement. Rewarded for their fixed personal union these select few shall put to use their inner compass combined with their professional leadership and highly skilled experience to contrive plans and navigate the global populations away from the Lord and in pursuit of Satan's visible material world. Antichrist's powerful right-hand authority figures shall be used to the Beast's advantage as leverage in transforming and creating the global population into the obeying image or statue of the Beast-Antichrist.

To briefly summarize Revelation 13:16. In the end, there are leaders and there are followers. It is not so much a physical mark only a psychological mark hidden in plain sight. Nevertheless with today's technological advancements it is possible to devise such a plan. And mingle both the physical and psychological marks inseparable. In which there is no escape.

Revelation 13:15 (King James Version) - "And he had power to give life unto the image of the Beast, that the image of the beast should both speak and cause that as many as would not worship the image of the beast, should be killed." The image of the Beast or the sea

of nations proclaim (with the guiding authority of the False Prophet) anyone not enthusiastically worshipping (supporting and obeying the new laws that govern) the Beast-Antichrist is immediately arrested, handed over to the proper right-hand authorities and prisoned and or to be executed, the Beast-Antichrist a deceiving tyrant who shall (as all royalty) demand reverence repeating the actions of worship from the past.

Revelation 13:17 (King James Version) - "And that no man might buy or sell, save he that had the mark or the name of the Beast, or the number of his name. Here is wisdom. Let him that hath understanding count the number of a man; and his number is six hundred threescore and six." That "no man" might buy or sell, or in other words people could not get involved in the world's economic affairs unless they have received the mark of the Beast-Antichrist unless they change their ways of thinking. The scripture also states: "save he" or preserve the individual who bare the spiritual mark or name of the Beast, or the number of his name may live to buy and sell. Surrendering in desperate fear their mortal life and eternal soul in favor of material gains. No matter what the consequences hold. Not only is the Antichrist the conqueror of what was thought to be the untouchable North American continent. He is looked upon as a miracle worker and savior who quickly and successfully retool the world's economic and political machine so that he is in complete charge allowing the global system to continue under his new laws.

The definition of mark: *characteristic.* The definition of characteristic: *constituting character; marking distinctive qualities-that which constitutes character.* The definition of character: *a mark engraved.*

The definition of engrave: *to imprint; to impress.* The definition of imprint: *to stamp; to fix on the mind or memory.* Taking the mark of the Beast-Antichrist starts with a change in thinking revealing in time noticeable changes in attitude, personality and conduct, adding up to a perfectly complete change of character. With evil's skillful power quickly chiseling away to create a new everlasting image of the Beast-Antichrist. Maintaining the shaping of one's thinking and forging of one's will by steady but gradual determine influence leaves a lasting impression.

The definition of name: *title.* The definition of title: *an inscription.* The definition of inscription: *the act of inscribing; words engraved.* This is in a spiritual sense leading back to taking the mark of the Beast. To engrave or to stamp or fix on the mind or memory, the spiritual mark of Antichrist's name and of his handy work. To put it simply: anything and everything an individual or individuals plan, carryout and or create permanently bears their name upon it. An invisible and yet visible inspired power that is far mightier than the creation itself. The Antichrist teaches and influences his evil methods to others the sea of nations with their own profound creative thoughts agreeably mimic the very reckless nature of the Beast shaping with evil's ever expanding frontiers an ugly worldwide scene offensive to Almighty God.

The definition of number: *to reckon; to enumerate.* The definition of enumerate: *to count number by number; to reckon or mention a number of things, each separately.* The definition of reckon: *to count; to estimate; to account, consider.* The definition of consider: *to fix the mind on; to ponder; to have respect to; to think seriously.* The definition of ponder: *to weigh in the mind; to consider; to deliberate.* The

definition of deliberate: *to weigh well in one's mind; to consider; to consult; to debate; to balance well in the mind; cautious; discreet; well advised.* The definition of discreet: *prudent; wary; judicious.* The definition of prudent: *provident; careful.* The definition of judicious: *sagacious.* The definition of sagacious: *quick of perception; shrewd; sage.* The definition of careful: *solicitous; cautious.* The definition of sage: *wise; well judged; of sound judgment.* The definition of solicitous: *anxious; very desirous; concerned; apprehensive.* The definition of apprehensive: *fearful; suspicious.*

With all the other definitions this set is applied in a spiritual sense physically manifesting with evil's own resurrection a finished product of loyal followers. It simply means each soul is scrutinized and openly studied proving worthy to become the Beast's property. A through deliberate pondering of each and every soul considered for citizenship an effectively shrewd apprehensive process to terminate any and all trouble makers who may disrupt the Beast's global system. Once a soul is accepted the completion of the spiritual contract ends with the personal sig-"nature" or name of the Beast-Antichrist a fellowship which is polished and refined with the profound everlasting seal of approval upon each new recruited and transformed soul. A complex process of perfection in selecting shaping and molding a complete society of worshippers (who fix and focus their minds and memory on the Antichrist) creating the entire image of the Beast.

Here is wisdom. Let him that hath understanding count the number of his name, and his name, and his number is six hundred three score and six. A score is the number twenty. Three score is sixty. The number of the man Antichrist is 666. The number 666 is symbolic of incompleteness in a spiritual nature, incomplete

to God. In contrast the number seven symbolizes completeness. The book of Revelations describes the seven churches, seven seals, seven trumpets, seven angels. The Pyramid of power (Revelation 13:11) known as the Unholy Trinity: Satan (6), Antichrist (6), False Prophet (6) collectively have fallen short of God's glory. This needs careful thought and prayer of understanding to solve this mystery. Nevertheless do not be discouraged and give up the quest for the Antichrist's identity. Perseverance has its own reward. Every creature no matter how small leaves a trail. He is much closer than you may think. The signs appear all around. One only needs to pay close attention. It is food for thought. I am hopeful this literature may assist in guiding you on a steady and stable course suitable for prayer and study.

Revelation 14:9-10 (King James Version) - "And the third angel followed them, saying with a loud voice, "If any man worship the beast and his image, and receive his mark in his forehead, or in his hand, the same shall drink of the wine of the wrath of God, which is poured out without mixture into the cup of his indignation; and he shall be tormented with fire and brimstone in the presence of the holy angels, and in the presence of the Lamb."

Revelation 14:11 (Modern Translation) - "The smoke of their torture rises forever and ever, and they will have no relief day or night, for they have worshiped the Creature and his statue, and have been tattooed with the code of his name."

The Rapture

Matthew 24:31-35 (Modern Translation) - "And I shall send forth my angels with the sound of a mighty trumpet blast, and they shall gather my chosen ones from the farthest ends of the earth and heaven. Now learn a lesson from the fig tree. When her branch is tender and the leaves begin to sprout, you know that summer is almost here. Just so, when you see all these things beginning to happen you can know that my return is near, even at the doors. Then at last this age will come to its close. Heaven and earth will disappear, but my words remain forever."

Matthew 24:31-35 (King James Version) - "And he shall send his angels with a great sound of a trumpet, and they shall gather together his elect from the four winds, from one end of heaven to the other. Now learn a parable of the fig tree; When his branch is yet tender, and put forth leaves, ye know that summer is nigh: So likewise ye, when ye shall see all these things, know that it is near, even at the doors. Verily I say unto you, this generation shall not pass, till all these things fulfilled."

There is one prophetic event most agree on, the return of the Messiah is close at hand. However, remember these two warnings: Matthew 24:36 (King James Version) - "But of that day and hour knoweth no man no, not the angels of heaven, but my father only." Matthew 24:42 (Modern Translation) - "So be prepared, for you don't know what day your Lord is coming." God will not reveal the exact moment of the Rapture or return to his only son, than no one knows. Acts 1:7 (Modern Translation) - "The Father sets those dates, he replied, and they are not for you to know."

Matthew 24:30 (Modern Translation) - "Immediately after the persecution of those days the sun will be darkened, and the moon will not give light and the stars will seem to fall from the heavens, and the powers overshadowing the earth will be convulsed. And then at last the "signal" of my coming will appear in the heavens and there will be deep mourning all around the earth." With every loss, there is a gain, and with every gain, there is a loss. God will not give the day and hour of our Lord's return, and yet God has given us signs to look out for. The Lord said the signal of his coming will appear. The definition of signal: *a sign to communicate intelligence, orders; at a distance; to communicate by signals-signs*. The signal or sign hung in the sky by God of our Lord's return is world war III. Immediately following the persecutions of the NWO, the aftermath of this devastating third world war quickly brings to life many dormant prophecies, the world's population living in deep fear under the terrible burden of the Beast-Antichrist. The natural disasters taking place the world over may continue to rapidly escalate in their intensity and frequency causing mankind to mourn and even curse God due their destructive power. The chastisements from God during the times of the Great Tribulation will be severe serving God in opening man's eyes from his spiritual sleep.

God the Father needs all to come to repentance. Some will take more persuading than others. Revelation 3:19 (Modern Translation) - "I continually discipline and punish everyone I love; so I must punish you, unless you turn from your indifference and become enthusiastic about the things of God." The reason for the dark period of the Great Tribulation is to bring rebellious man to full repentance and to humble and

persuade those to live good godly lives. In the case of Jonah, if God cannot get through to mankind one way, he may use a more harsh method.

The gospel of the good new continues to spread around the globe. Matthew 24:14 (Modern Translation) - "And the Good News about the Kingdom will be preached throughout the whole world, so that all nations will hear it, and then finally The End will come." Ever since the good news of the Lord Jesus was revealed to the world following his crucifixion and resurrection. The teachings of the Gospel have painstakingly spread throughout the earth in a gentle and yet powerful display of God's great will. Despite many persecutions and sacrifices, God's will has grown stronger and wide known, today in these last days, when God is satisfied that he has done all he can to try and persuade mankind to repent using this gentle method. Then at the appropriate time God uses a stronger method. God allows The End (meaning the end of this age man is presently experiencing) times to give birth to the Great Tribulation (at the start of the NWO and third world war). And during this period shall be mankind's last chance to repent of his sins. When again God is satisfied that he has done all he could to persuade as many to repent as possible using these stronger methods. Then at God's appointed time (a moment in time the Father knows alone) he will send forth his son. The Lord Jesus then sends forth the heavenly angels to gather the harvest of chosen souls immediately following the third world war and prior to the final battle of Armageddon. The natural plagues (described in the book of Revelation) shall be thrown upon the earth to bring rebellious mankind to one final chance at repentance. During these turbulent times of many natural disasters and much human

misery the Rapture takes place in the blink of an eye, inevitably leading to the final Battle, the destruction of the Antichrist and his vast military empire.

Revelation 7:9 (Modern Translation) - "After this I saw a vast crowd too great to count from all nations and provinces and languages, standing in front of the throne and before the Lamb, clothed in white, with palm branches in their hands." Revelation 7:13-14 (Modern Translation) - "Then one of the twenty-four elders asked me, "Do you know who these are, who are clothed in white, and where they come from?" "No sir, I replied. Please tell me." These are the ones coming out of the Great Tribulation, he said, they washed their robes and whitened them by the blood of the Lamb." This vast crowd from every nation and province and language is the harvest of souls gathered together. These are the ones Coming out of the Great Tribulation from the farthest reaches of heaven and all over the earth. These blessed souls are the chosen who participated in the Rapture.

There is only two ways that I have learned that may help you escape these coming horrors. The first is to flee from the Western Hemisphere and stay away. The second is: Luke 21:36 (Modern Translation) - "Keep a constant watch. And pray that if possible you may arrive in my presence without having to experience these horrors." The scripture reveals to stay alert (holding tightly to your crown of life) and keep a constant watch upon the many developing prophetical signs taking place and pray alone "WITHOUT TAKING MATTERS OF SELF DESTRUCTION INTO YOUR OWN HANDS" for your passing before

these judgments strike. Ask and pray with patience and reverence.

<u>Luke 18:6-7</u> (Modern Translation) - "Then the Lord said, "If even an evil judge can be worn down like that, don't you think that God will surely give justice to his people who plead with him day and night?

A Warning

Isaiah 47:11 (Modern Translation) - "That is why disaster shall overtake you suddenly-so suddenly that you won't know where it comes from. And there will be no atonement then to cleanse away your sins."

Jeremiah 51:6 (Modern Translation) - "Flee from Babylon! Save yourself! Don't get trapped! If you stay, you will be destroyed when God takes his vengeance on all Babylon's sins."

Revelation 18:4 (Modern Translation) - "Then I heard another voice calling from heaven "Come away from her, my people; do not take part in her sins, or you will be punished with her."

The cloak concealing the identity of this mysterious Babylon has now been unveiled to you. With that message comes an important warning from the Lord to all concerned, an urgent bell ringer that is woven into the fabric of her prophetic future unwise to ignore.

In the three scriptures above, the Lord has commanded his people (Jews and Gentiles alike) to leave the Great Babylon before God's terrible judgments strike her down as Lot and his family were warned to leave the land of Sodom and Gomorrah and their neighboring towns before their destruction. The Lord today is now warning all his people of this Modern Babylon and her neighboring nations to clear out of the Western Hemisphere not only because of

the soon to be third world war's terrible destruction and much loss of life. The souls of many will perish in eternal dam nation. The very place many of the souls of Sodom and Gomorrah and their neighbors went following their judgment.

Isaiah 14:9-11 (Modern Translation) - "The denizens of hell crowd to meet you as you enter their domain. World leaders and earth's mightiest kings, long dead, are there to see you. With one voice they all cry out, "Now you are as weak as we are!" Your might and power are gone; they are buried with you. All the pleasant music in your palace has ceased; now maggots are your sheet, worms your blanket!" The Lord has spoken plainly. There will be "NO ATONEMENT" then to cleanse away your sins. The definition of atonement: *reconciliation; satisfaction*. The definition of reconciliation: *act of reconciling; a renewal of friendship*. There will be "NO RENEWAL OF FRIENDSHIP" at the start of the third world war on that day of her judgment between God and the people of the Modern Babylon and her neighboring nations.

The sad truth, as Lot's wife many without hesitation will choose to disobey God regardless of the Lord's pleas and warnings. For the simple reason they love their lives more than they love God. And will pay the ultimate price for their actions.

It would be very unwise for all concern to neglect these warnings from the Lord. But there are always those who think they can ride out the storm and survive. Or have the relaxed reassurance that it won't happen in their life time. Think again! No matter what you do, or who you are, Jew and Gentile alike. If you choose to ignore one of the most important messages

in modern times from the Lord and take your chances. The Lord will take it as a simple "NO." And you will perish. And yes, it can happen to you. Take my advice and heed the warnings. Allow an abundance of thought and prayer to seriously reconsider your position with the Lord. Leave the Western Hemisphere while there is still time. The sand in the hour glass is running out.

THE WRITING ON THE WALL

Today many believe America will never perish from the earth. They have the same misconception towards America that was created with the ocean liner Titanic. Conceiving the notion America is a luxurious unsinkable ship built to withstand any and all situations.

When the Antichrist commence with the third world war, America will descend into an ocean of nuclear fire. Dragging many misguided souls down with her. At the appropriate time the Locusts are then unleashed in a rampaging blitzkrieg with mass formations of men and material devouring everyone and everything before them. America is the one sending out the "S"ave "O"ur "S"ouls distress signal. The thought of a third world war to engulf the sole superpower United States is often difficult to imagine a nation appearing to have every angle of preparation in defense of national security. Nevertheless, revived cold war tensions between the east and west once again appear to be on the rise. Complicated political issues with debates taking shape have created what has long been dread, another arms race.

THE COLD WAR

Daniel 11:27 (Modern Translation) - "Both these kings will be plotting against each other at the conference table, attempting to deceive each other. But it will

make no difference, for neither can succeed until God's appointed time has come."

Daniel 2:43 (Modern Translation) - "This mixture of iron with clay also shows that these kingdoms will try to strengthen themselves by forming alliances with each other through intermarriage of their rulers; but this will not succeed, for iron and clay don't mix."

Daniel 11:40 (King James Version) - "And at the time of the end shall the king of the south push at him; and the king of the north shall come against him like a whirlwind, with chariots, and with horsemen, and with many ships; and he shall enter into the countries, and shall overflow and pass over."

Studying a world map I observed the geographic location of the continental United States is directly south in latitude to Russia's most southern border. The three scriptures available is a brief description of the cold war between two powerful kings meeting at the agreed peace conferences each with their own strategic ways of deceit. Beneath the tense polite talks, warm smiles and hardy handshakes the two opposing sides were never close allies as the leaders claim. The walls of mutual suspicion in place to create the long standing cold war were never taken down. And these "kingdoms" attempt to sort out their differences through a New World Order of alliance, and will not succeed. For iron and clay do not mix. Their views on worldly affairs are in contrast with one another.

Even before the heat up of the cold war, the U.S. suspected Russia as a growing menace to America's plans for global security and peace. The seeds sown at the beginning to create such a long standing conflict

were: pride, arrogance, paranoia, ignorance, greed, and prejudice to name a few. These small unseen sins hidden in the minds of powerful wealthy leaders grew in many tragic ways. Complexes creating these gaps basically widen by brainwashing and conditioning the peoples of both sides to mistrust and hate each other. This in turn created division ranging from the splitting of families, and generations, to single countries, continents and even the Eastern and Western Hemisphere. As the years went by many defense lines were drawn. Battle strategies planned and executed. Covert and black operations went into effect. Leaders became military dictators suppressing and driving their peoples into famine and hopelessness. Leading to crime and violence, wide spread diseases, and international terrorism compounding the world problems to new heights of disorder.

The cold war between the two countries inevitably gave birth to the arms race at which the United States began her political ideological practices and military offensive and defensive stance - "pushing" or manipulate, provoke and at certain times attack the Russians. Causing endless tensions and concerns throughout the globe of American dominance and power. Fear is America's motivation over Russia's enormous land mass and strategic geographic elevation housing ever increasing political/military influence and power. Historical wars with Napoleon's French Empire and Hitler's Nazi Germany have proven the Russians are at their most dangerous when their back is against the wall. Nevertheless America's methods of use and abuse of political and or military power pushing is an act of aggression and considered an act of war. In these last days may reveal very dangerous practices.

The Road to Ruin

Revelation 17:16 (Modern Translation) - "The Scarlet Animal and his ten horns - which represent ten kings who will reign with him - all hate the woman, and will attack her and leave her naked and ravaged by fire."

Jeremiah 51:14 (Modern Translation) - "The Lord Almighty has taken this vow and sworn to it in his own name: Your cities shall be filled with enemies, like fields with locusts in a plague and they shall lift to the skies their mighty shouts of victory."

The discovery of nuclear energy was a dark period in human history like no other inevitably, leading the nations towards an arms race that would dominate world politics for decades. And the cold war is more or less a Mexican standoff with both sides spending trillions on countless military and civilian projects in research and weapons development. Over time, mankind's hunger to gain the material advantage over each other increased. His technological advances began to slowly rebuild and modernize his civilization. And western technological breakthroughs fan the flames of corruption and mad obsession with superior power. In which international tensions and hostility began to mount and steadily worsen. Early on suspicions were confirmed and many realized war between the East and the West was evident. It is crystal clear many view this long standoff as did Nostradamus. "Mankind will increase the way in which he waged war as he improves his technology."

Century II, Quatrain 89:
One day the two great masters shall be friends,

their great powers shall be increased,
the new land shall be in a flourishing condition,
the number shall be told to the bloody person.

The two great masters, Russia and America shall be friends or in my view estranged allies. Over the course of time their national powers have been on a dramatic increase. The new land of America has been in a tremendous flourishing condition. The number of days until the third world war is in a master plan of the bloody person or Antichrist.

Two prophecies which reveal America's fiery destruction and invasion to follow and since there is none higher in authority than God, Jehovah swore by his own holy name the horrible war will come to pass. These warnings have been carved in stone and should be taken very seriously. For those individuals who ignore history are condemned to repeat it. The one history lesson continually ignored: "Mankind has never created a weapon he has not used." There is but one use and purpose for all weapons of war total submission and or annihilation of the enemy.

On July 16, 2001 Russia and China signed treaty of friendship and co-operation permanently cementing a partnership between the two nations. "Apparently the two eastern giants are concerned with the growing influence of the United States. And have agreed to promote their interests by committing them to jointly oppose much of the framework for international security and peace that the United States is seeking to erect." The framework for international security is the motivation binding the two eastern giants together.

America who remains vigilant with the war on terror and the standing alliance between Russia and China revived cold war tensions. With a new arms race underway, my "prediction" tensions will escalate nearly out of control to the point of near all-out war. Nevertheless events will be contained. Both sides reach agreements laying the foundation for the New World Order. A frail global security of peace (iron mixed with clay) when the nations witness the formal treaty of world peace. Those who are spiritually prepared will see the truth. A warning of impending danger may flash out across the minds of those who are spiritually awake. The nations of the earth will be entering through the doorway of a new age the age of the Antichrist. And once through the door it will slam shut. There will be no turning back. Then all the prophecies described will follow.

Under martial law of the NWO, I foresee a distressing time in the United States of strife and civil unrest worse than any previous in American history creating her present gradual and steady decay into a relentless incessant decline. Were mankind confronts the locked door of despair, God discovers a window of opportunity. When America experiences the loss of liberty, the suppression may begin to awaken the spirit of the grieving. With all hopes and efforts to restore righteousness crushed including witnessing for themselves the moral decline of the United States. The golden opportunity for many will have arrived to once again turn to the Lord encouraging God's people to leave the West prior to the fulfillment of the holy prophecies.

It is interesting to note, in the epistle to King Henry II, Nostradamus briefly wrote about the procreation of a new Babylon, "A miserable prostitute large with abomination." Revelation 17:5 (King James Version) - "And upon her forehead was a name written, MYSTERY, BABYLON THE GREAT, THE

MOTHER OF HARLOTS AND ABOMINATIONS OF THE EARTH." The definition of abomination: *hatred; object of hatred; loathsomeness.* The United States has become an object of hatred and disgust all over the earth. Revelation 18:2 (Modern Translation) – "He gave a mighty shout, "Babylon the Great is fallen, is fallen; she has become a den of demons, a haunt of devils and every kind of evil spirit." The first fallen, Babylon – the United States of America has spiritually and morally fallen identical to the decline of the Roman Empire, rotting away from within which shall inevitably lead to her second fallen. She will fall to destruction with nuclear fire similar to the judgment of Sodom and Gomorrah. World powers are working furiously in preparation for an all-out attack. The winds of many tactical advantages once in America's favor now shift against her. Powerful heads of state have a common agenda with a guiding compass of profound hidden resentments toward her and it is the seeds of resentment amass together in their minds creating and shaping a planned road map of world domination, unknowingly inscribing an open invitation for the Antichrist to gain their complete trust of fellowship. With the Antichrist's arrival they shall all agree to combine their collective powers together to reap America's destruction. In a humiliating defeat America the beautiful shall fall to the poor. Reasons enough perhaps for World War III, is inevitable and it shall be America's Last Stand.

Final Thoughts

The prophets of the past foretold a great tribulation in the end times would shake the very foundation of this world. In these last days ordinary people worldwide

are clearly witnessing many astounding events coming to pass. The signs appear all around. The United States particularly has been warned of incoming disaster for years from enviromentalists, scientists, religious leaders, and a small number of politicians to name a few. In contrast many tend to believe the horrible judgment described would never rain down upon the United States due to the impressive heights of enormous political, economic and military power The popular belief the modern technological wonders and achievements of man's design are proof enough he has gained divine province everlasting favor. Basking in false security, the voice of their ignorance grows louder.

History teaches no matter how invincible a nation or kingdom may appear. There always comes along another that is greater. Constantly in a never ending cycle man stalks one another with promises of victory creating a vicious and twisted game king of the mountain inevitably leading to the deadly consequences of bloodshed and war. And war in all its false hopes of glory will not necessarily destroy evil. It only suppresses it for a while until it comes back in full fury. And mankind has advanced to the point of no return it has become evident mankind cannot stop progress. Progress will one day stop him.

It has been said "Success can test faith as any adversary." When a nation, in the full bloom of prosperity rejects God the inevitable end result is ruin. The one fatal recurring blunder man has made throughout history. He was never meant to govern himself. In the final analysis the technological era we find ourselves in is now and will be to come disastrous for the whole earth. It is God alone who shall reveal to all mankind beyond a shadow of any doubt the true master of this house.

There is a Chinese proverb: "Give a man a fish, you feed him for a day. Teach a man to fish you feed him for life." What I offer is a small eye opening contribution to the world study of prophecy, attempting to provide from the inner guiding compass of basic God given common sense the biblical understanding for the coming years. A grim realistic scared straight tactic so many may heed the warnings. In learning the set timetable of events I began to understand God (in a gradual steady manner) is planning, revealing and executing each prophetic event in stages thereby allowing mankind enough time between each catastrophic trial to reach a final life or death decision to justly benefit his people for his everlasting glory. How I have come to understand the Great Tribulation it is the greatest-storm in human history testing everyone alive. The birth-pains of events (in their proper order) within God's prophetic calendar consist of: 1. The New World Order (and the recognition of the ten horns or ten king rise to power). 2. The arrival of the Antichrist and the appearance of the two heavenly witnesses. 3. World War III and the destruction of the Mighty Babylon. 4. The aftermath of the third world war and the rule of the Antichrist. 5. The trials and plagues in all their natural disasters. 6. The Rapture of the harvest. 7. The final battle and the destruction of the Antichrist and his vast military empire. It is a mighty storm currently gathering strength on the horizon. So I now pass the torch of knowledge to you, a gift not only to you the reader, the entire world. The power of knowledge that I hope may inspire and lead you to the path of more profound wisdom. There is much to think about. Use the time wisely. Remember, "He who hesitates is his loss." In these last days, time is far more valuable than gold.

What I have attempted to provide is a basic understanding of each major event shaping and creating the dark period of the Great Tribulation. Now it is your turn to pick up where I left off with more in-depth study and learning. And with sincere profound thought you shall learn the Lord is the key to eternal knowledge and wisdom. Awaken the dormant powers from within with the "careful" prayer of understanding. Pay strict attention to detail as you learn to read between the lines, spend some time and meditate upon each prophetic chapter with profound thought and prayer. Answers will come when you are patient and still enough to receive them. Remember the experience brings forth knowledge as any past or present situation you are or have been involved with. This is the right time of history for this work. Remember George Bernard Shaw wrote: "Beware of false knowledge, it is more dangerous than ignorance." Use your God given knowledge and experiences "in earnest and not deceit" to benefit and inspire mankind to live peaceful holy lives preparing for our Lord's return. And may the Lord guide your every step.

Reviewing all that has been learned over the years, I have reasoned through all the trials and tribulations in my life. Salvation is the scale of perfection that balances out the weights of knowledge and wisdom. With this in mind, the most important lesson I have learned is love, mostly love for God the Father is truly the greatest of all.

The Truth Will Set You Free!

To be forewarn, is to be forearmed

CPSIA information can be obtained at www.ICGtesting.com
Printed in the USA
LVOW04s2049230815

451224LV00021B/543/P

9 780741 473462